DEADLINE

DEADLINE

by

Vernon Coleman

with best wishes

[signature]

Chilton Designs

First published in the United Kingdom, 1994,
by Chilton Designs Publishers,
Preston House, Kentisbury, Barnstaple, Devon EX31 4NH, England.
Copyright Vernon Coleman 1994

A catalogue record for this book is available from the British Library.

All characters and places in this publication are fictitious and any resemblance
to real persons, living or dead, is purely coincidental.

ISBN: 1 898146–10–1

Printed in Great Britain at The Bath Press, Avon

CHAPTER 1

It hadn't been the best week I'd ever had.

On Monday I'd lost my job. Actually, that's a euphemism. I hadn't 'lost' my job at all. I knew exactly where it was. The simple truth is that on Monday I'd been fired.

On Tuesday my wife had walked out on me. No warning. No explanation. Just packed her bags and gone. I'd got back from a training session at the gym and found that she'd taken everything from the flat that either belonged to her or was of any value. She hadn't even left a note.

On Wednesday morning I lay awake in bed trying not to think of either of those things and struggling to get back to sleep. When I heard the little click that the alarm clock always makes a second or so before it starts to ring I reached over and switched it off. There wasn't much point in getting up early; there wasn't much to get out of bed for. The day was likely to be long enough as it was.

My world had fallen apart at 9.35 am on Monday when the managing editor had told me that the paper was, with reluctance, 'going to have to let me go.'

'It'll give you an opportunity to stretch your talents elsewhere,' he'd said, without even blushing. I wondered if I'd have liked it more if he'd been blunt about it. 'We don't like you. You're fired. Get out. Life's tough.' Probably not.

I knew why they'd done it.

For six years I'd been the paper's chief investigative reporter. As long as I confined myself to writing about the sort of crooks who wore masks and carried sledge hammers they'd been happy. But I'd written too many stories about financial crime in the city and they hadn't gone down well with the paper's owners. To avoid any confusion I ought to make it clear that it was my stories that hadn't gone down well. The crimes hadn't gone down badly at all.

To begin with there had been a few subtle warnings. The news editor had sent me up to Manchester to cover a murder trial. I'd spent two weeks there and had sent back about fifteen thousand words of copy. They'd used two paragraphs and one of those had been from an agency reporter.

But I've never been very good at taking hints. When I got back to London I carried on doing some research into computer fraud in one of the City's leading banks. When the news editor had told me that they couldn't use the story I'd passed the information I'd acquired on to the police.

That hadn't really been a bright career move. The man who'd founded the paper just happened to be a director of the bank.

I'd known that when I'd started the story but I've always been a stubborn bastard.

I was still a stubborn bastard, but now I was an unemployed stubborn bastard.

I shuffled out of the bedroom into the kitchenette. I love the way estate agents make up words like 'kitchenette'. It sounds sweet and neat. In fact it means that even they are embarrassed to call six square feet of space a kitchen. I gulped down a glass of orange juice and staggered back into the bedroom. I rummaged around on the floor by the side of the bed until I found my grey tracksuit. Finding my running shoes took longer. One shoe was under the bed and the other was half buried under a pile of dirty washing. I was beginning to live like a slob. It wasn't out of character. I felt like a slob.

The three mile run round the park woke me up but it didn't make me feel any better about myself or the future. Apart from breakfast I didn't have any plans for the future. I cooked mushrooms, tomatoes, scrambled eggs and vegetarian sausages. I gave up eating dead animals three years ago.

I made breakfast last as long as possible. I read the morning papers, made toast under the grill and drank two large cups of black coffee. The smell of the coffee and the toast should have made me feel better but it didn't. At ten I finished the crossword. The only thing left to read in the paper was the page listing the share prices and I wasn't quite that desperate. I dumped the dirty dishes in the sink and wandered back into the bedroom. I had planned to get changed but I'd only got one clean shirt and I thought I'd better keep that in case I really needed it.

I shrugged, wiped a blob of marmalade from the front of my tracksuit and headed for the door. I had to get out. I didn't know where. Just out. The postman had delivered two bills and a bank statement. I tossed them onto the table in the hall. I knew exactly how much I'd got in the bank without looking.

As I left the phone started to ring. I ignored it. I couldn't think of anyone in the world I wanted to speak to. I suddenly realised that since I'd left the paper I hadn't spoken to a single, living soul. Unless you count a few words to the checkout girl at the local supermarket.

Downstairs in the underground car park I found that someone had slipped a note underneath the windscreen wipers of my car. It was the usual threatening note from the insurance broker who lives in Flat 3D and is chairman of our building's Residents' Committee. He pointed out that my car overhung my parking bar by 17 inches and that it was a potential inconvenience to other residents. I crumpled the note up and tossed it into a nearby litter basket.

My car is a steel grey Bentley S1. I bought it three years ago with money I earned from a book about mass murderers. It was built in 1958 for a long forgotten and recently dead actor who had more taste than talent. I bought it partly because I liked it, partly because it was a bargain I couldn't refuse and partly because I thought it was probably a good investment. I've never been much good with money. There isn't any point in my putting money into a bank or building society account. I just draw it out the following week and spend it. But I knew that I wouldn't sell the car unless I became desperate.

As I slipped the key into the lock I wondered how long it would be before I became that desperate. The red leather seats were cracking with age but they still felt firm and comfortable. And, as always, the engine started first time. The car needed servicing every 2,500 miles but it was worth it. It cost me a fortune in garage bills and the 4.8 litre engine rarely managed more than 12 miles to the gallon but it never let me down.

I drove down St John's Wood Road, past Lord's cricket

ground, and turned left heading for Baker Street. The roads around London are so clogged with traffic these days that it is usually quicker to drive straight through the centre of the city. Everyone else expects the city centre to be one big traffic jam so they keep well away.

The gym I usually use is in South London, on the other side of the river. It's unfashionable, dirty and patronised almost exclusively by fighters or would-be fighters. I'd never found a better way of keeping fit than working out at a gym with young, tough, aspiring professional boxers. They aren't there because it's fashionable to work out or because they want to look good; they are there because they are hungry for success.

About two years ago I tried one of the new, smart city gyms that have sprung up to cater for businessmen who want to keep fit. I paid my several hundred pounds membership fee and went there twice. There was plenty of shiny, chromium-plated equipment but I didn't feel comfortable there. I like my work-outs to be real not superficial. I walked out of the smart gym when I heard two guys who were supposed to be training discussing the price of copper. In a real gym no one talks. They may grunt occasionally but they don't talk. Anger and sweat are the two most vital ingredients for a good work-out and there was very little of either in the upmarket city gym.

I parked the car on the piece of wasteland that adjoins the gym and gave Johnny a couple of coins to keep an eye on it. Johnny is about sixty and used to be a fighter. His brain was slightly scrambled when he prolonged his career by one fight too many but he's still lean and hard and the local kids don't mess with him. He always hangs around so that he can look after cars. I gave Johnny the keys so that he could sit in the car if it rained.

I was about ten feet from the door to the gym when I heard someone call my name.

I turned and saw someone I vaguely remembered standing by a small BMW on the other side of the road. He wore a blue two piece suit with a white silk shirt and a cricket club tie that I recognised. He had one arm half raised, presumably to attract my attention. It wasn't really necessary. The road where the gym was situated isn't exactly heavily populated. There was no one else in sight.

4

'Mark Watson?' he said, holding his jacket together as he ran across the road. 'My name's Michael Sunderland, I'm sorry to bother you.'

The ten yards run seemed to have winded him. He was in his late twenties but already had a noticeable paunch. It was, however, his eyes which caught my attention. They looked hollow. He looked haunted and exhausted.

I took his outstretched hand and shook it gently. It felt plump and podgy.

'Can I talk to you?' he asked, breathlessly. 'It's very important.'

'Sure.' I remembered why I knew him. He worked in the advertising department of the paper I'd just left.

He looked around. 'Is there somewhere we can go?'

'There's a café two hundred yards up the road.' I told him. The only people who used it were the guys from the gym. None of them were likely to be there at this time of day.

Sunderland pulled his car keys out of his trouser pocket and started to head back across the road towards his BMW. I caught his arm.

'Let's walk,' I said. I waved to Johnny and signalled for him to keep an eye on the BMW as well.

Neither of us spoke during the walk to the café. Once inside I ordered two large mugs of tea and two plates of bread and butter. The owner doesn't like people going in there just for a drink. We sat in silence until the drinks and the food came.

'I hope you don't mind my coming to you,' began Sunderland. He tried to pick up his mug of tea but his hands were shaking too much. He put it down again quickly.

'What's the problem?' I asked. 'Why me?'

'I didn't know who else to go to.'

I picked up a slice of bread and butter, folded it in half and bit a chunk out of it. George uses ordinary thick sliced white bread and unsalted butter but his bread and butter always tastes better than anyone else's. I've never understood why.

'Peter Norton suggested I talk to you.'

I recognised the name. Peter Norton is one of the paper's staff lawyers. He's more than an acquaintance and not quite a friend.

5

I put three large spoons of sugar into my tea and stirred it carefully.

'I don't know where to start.'

Suddenly, I noticed that he had tears in his eyes. It was a long time since I'd seen another man cry. I looked down feeling uncomfortable. I know crying is supposed to be really healthy but it always embarrasses the hell out of me. 'Start at the beginning,' I told him. I've always been an original thinker.

He licked his lips and took a deep breath. It was clearly all a tremendous effort. I didn't know how to make it easier for him. I just waited.

'I got married ten days ago,' he blurted out suddenly. 'I married a girl called Barbara. You might have seen her. She works in the classified ads department.'

I tried to place her.

'Blonde, about five foot ten, always dresses well. Very pretty.'

I nodded. I'd seen her. It wasn't too difficult to remember her. She was more than just pretty.

'Beautiful girl. You're a lucky fellow.'

He nodded and tried to pick up his mug again. His hands were still shaking too much for him to hold it.

'Go on.' I said, after a few moments silence.

'We went to Paris for our honeymoon. It was marvellous. The most wonderful time of my life. Everything was perfect. The hotel. The weather. The food.'

I started to say something about it not being perfect if he'd noticed the weather but stopped myself just in time. I'm not often tactful and I felt proud of myself.

'Three days ago it was time to come back. We had about an hour to go before we needed to catch the bus to the airport so we went to the Café de la Paix near to the Opera for a last coffee.'

I nodded. I knew it well.

'We'd left our luggage at the hotel and were planning to get a taxi up to the bus depot at the top of the Champs d'Elysée and pick up our bags on the way.'

I nodded again.

'I ordered the coffees and then decided to go to the loo before we set off for the airport.' His whole body was shaking now. I reached out and put a hand on his arm.

'I wasn't away more than a couple of minutes at the most,' he went on. 'When I got back Barbara was gone.' Tears began to roll down his cheeks.

'At first I just thought I must have mistaken the table,' he went on. 'Then I thought that maybe she had slipped off to the ladies. Or gone outside to buy a newspaper or a magazine from the kiosk on the pavement.'

'But she didn't come back?'

He shook his head. 'I asked around,' he said. 'But the only person who remembered her was a German woman. She said she'd seen Barbara leave with another man. She said he was about medium height, heavy build, balding and wore a thick tweed overcoat.' He paused. 'I asked her for a good description in case it was someone I knew.'

'But it wasn't?'

He shook his head again. There was a lot of nodding and shaking going on.

'So, what did you do then?'

'I still half expected her to reappear,' said Sunderland. 'It all seemed like a nightmare. I couldn't think what could have happened or where she could have gone.'

I could see that he was making a real effort not to break down completely.

'I waited at the café for another half an hour and then I went to a telephone, called the airport and told them that we wouldn't be making the flight.'

I nodded encouragement. He needed it.

'The German woman who'd seen Barbara leave said she'd gone willingly with the man in the tweed overcoat after he'd told her something that had made her cry,' Sunderland said. 'I couldn't understand any of it. I couldn't understand why she'd left, why she hadn't left me a note, why she didn't come back.'

'What did you do then?'

'I went back to the hotel. Our cases were still behind the receptionist's desk where we'd left them. But no one had seen Barbara. I managed to re-book a room for the night and left a message there for Barbara in case she showed up. Then I raced back to the café and left a message for her there too. I tried

7

giving the message to one of the waiters but he suggested I taped a note to her onto the glass doors at the front of the café.'

'I take it that she still hasn't turned up?' I said. 'You haven't heard from her at all?'

He shook his head.

'How long did you wait in Paris?'

'Another 24 hours. I tried the police, the British Embassy and the local hospitals. I tried everyone I could think of.'

'What did the police say?'

'They didn't seem very interested.'

'What about the Embassy?'

'The same. Everyone seemed to think I was making a fuss about nothing. They all said that I should just go home and that she'd probably turn up in a few days.'

'How long had you known Barbara before you got married?'

'Two years,' he answered. 'We'd lived together for six months.'

'What made you get married?'

He blushed. 'We wanted to start a family.'

'As far as you know did she have any friends in Paris?'

'She'd never been to France before. She didn't even speak French.'

'Had you met anyone while you were over there?'

He shook his head. 'We were on our honeymoon,' he reminded me. 'We didn't want to be with anyone else. We didn't even go on any of the coach tours that were part of the trip.'

'Did she have any money with her when she disappeared?'

'The police wanted to know that. She had 50 or 60 pounds I think. Mostly in sterling.'

'Did she have her passport?'

He nodded.

'Did she suffer from any health problems? Epilepsy? Diabetes? Anything like that?'

'No. Nothing.'

'And the hospitals hadn't admitted anyone answering her description?'

Another shake of the head. 'I actually managed to get someone from the Embassy to ring round all the hospitals that I hadn't been able to check. But there was nothing.'

'When did you get back to London?'

'The day before yesterday. In the evening. As soon as I got back I rang round her friends in London. No one had heard anything. Then I telephoned the police. They said that since it happened in Paris it was nothing to do with them.'

'And then you went to see Peter Norton?'

Another nod. 'He's a good friend. I've known him for years.'

Why did he suggest you talked to me?'

'He said we had to consider the possibility that she might have been kidnapped. He said you knew more about crime and criminals than anyone else he knew.' He paused. 'He said I could trust you.'

'Have you received a ransom note?'

'No.'

'Nothing at all?'

'Nothing.'

'Did Peter tell you that you could find me here?'

'He gave me your phone number, your home address and this address. I tried to ring you last night and this morning but there was no reply. So I came here.'

I picked up my mug and took a long, slow drink from it. 'Can you think of anyone who would want to kidnap her?'

'No.' He paused. 'We don't have enough money to make it worth anyone's while.' He said it as though he was slightly embarrassed.

'You don't have rich parents?'

'My father is a painter and decorator in Reading. He and my mother live in a semidetached house.'

'What about your wife's parents?'

He shook his head. 'Barbara's parents aren't rich either.'

'Have you any enemies?'

'Enemies?' He seemed startled by the question.

'Anyone who would want to harm you?'

'No.'

'Has Barbara?'

'No, of course not.'

I took another bite out of the slice of bread and butter and washed it down with a gulp of sweet tea.

Across the table Michael Sunderland took out a linen handkerchief and noisily blew his nose. It was a long time since I'd

9

seen anyone use anything other than a piece of crumpled tissue for nose blowing. 'I just don't know what to do,' he said, very softly. He looked forlorn and lonely; a bewildered and frightened man who had, probably for the first time in his life, come into contact with the dark realities of the world. He looked straight at me; his plump pink cheeks tear stained and his eyes lifeless and almost empty of hope. 'I don't know what to do,' he said quietly. 'Will you help me?'

I didn't know what to do either but it was easier for me to stay tough and sound optimistic.

'Yeah,' I promised. 'I'll try.'

CHAPTER TWO

I didn't know where to start so I sent Sunderland back home and told him I'd ring him later. Then, I went into the gym to think.

Two hours later, in the shower, I realized that all I'd thought about was the job I didn't have and the wife who'd left me. I knew which I'd miss most. And knew that was probably one of the reasons why she'd left me. The other reason would be money. She liked having money. She wouldn't have liked not having any. I wondered where she'd gone. The last I knew she had a choice of two. A banker or a solicitor. Both loaded.

I'd enjoyed my job. And I knew I'd miss it. I also knew that I'd probably never get another like it. These days newspaper owners don't want investigative journalists. Too many investigations upset the advertisers. The funny thing is that if I hadn't enjoyed my job so much, and hadn't been so good at it, I probably wouldn't have lost it.

I came out of the shower and found Billy waiting for me. Everyone who hangs around real gyms knows that there's a rule that people who work there have to have names with a 'y' on the end. Billy didn't say anything but held one huge fist next to his ear as though he was about to punch himself on the side of the head.

Billy isn't a great talker but at six foot five he's an inch or so taller than me and at seventeen and a half stone he's a good three stones heavier too. If he doesn't want to talk a lot that's fine by me. Billy was a contender who missed his chance at the title after his manager got greedy. Still, he got the gym out of a career that went on too long. And he always seemed happier than most of the people I know.

It was Sunderland on the phone. He was excited and spoke

so fast I could hardly hear what he said. I asked him to slow down a bit and waggled my index finger around in my ear to try and get some of the soapy water out.

'I've just had a phone call,' he said. 'I think it's them.'

'Them?'

'The people who've kidnapped Barbara.'

I was surprised. I hadn't really taken to the kidnapping theory. I still half suspected that Sunderland's wife had just walked out on him. I knew that was something that some wives did.

'They want to meet me this afternoon.'

'Who's they?'

'A woman.'

'What did she say?'

'Just that she'd booked a table for two at The Grand. Five o'clock for tea.'

I almost laughed. And then I realized it probably wasn't so daft after all. Crowds of people. Public place.

'What else did she say?'

'Just that she knew Barbara would want me to meet her and that the table was booked in the name of Reynolds.'

'So we know one thing about her.'

'What?' Sunderland sounded excited and I felt guilty.

'Her name isn't Reynolds.' I said. 'Cuts it down a bit.' I pulled the towel around me a little tighter and stamped my feet. Billy's only telephone is stuck in a freezing hallway. I looked down at my bare feet and wondered how blue toes had to go before they were irreversibly damaged. 'Did she mention the police?'

'She said I wasn't to contact them.'

'Don't.' I said. I peered round the doorway into Billy's office. The huge clock on the wall said twenty past two. 'Do exactly what she said,' I told him. 'I'll be there too.' I hung up and went to get dressed.

CHAPTER THREE

I poured myself another cup of tea, nibbled at an egg and cress sandwich and wondered how much this was going to cost me. I wondered if it was bad form to ask for expenses while doing a favour for a friend of an acquaintance. I didn't mind forking out for tea and bread and butter at the café near the gym but I had an overpowering suspicion that I was going to have to take out a loan on the Bentley to pay for tea at The Grand.

It had cost me a tenner and a favour to get the table. Like most big cities, London operates on the favour system. It's favours not money that make the world go round. I didn't know the head waiter at The Grand but I knew the barman quite well and he put in a good word for me. Without his help not even money would have got me in. American and Japanese tourists book up to take tea at The Grand in their hundreds. Watching the guardsmen change places at Buckingham Palace just down the road is thirsty work.

I'd booked my table for 4.30 pm. I wanted plenty of time to see if I could spot anyone who looked as if she was pretending to be called Reynolds when her name was really something else.

Michael Sunderland turned up at 5 pm as instructed. I watched as he introduced himself to the head waiter and asked to be shown to Ms Reynolds' table. He was sweating profusely and kept mopping his brow with his handkerchief.

As I stuffed myself with egg and cress I noticed that the head waiter seemed to be bringing Sunderland over in my direction. I looked around. On my left sat two elderly English ladies who were deep in loud conversation about something awful that had happened in Cheltenham and seemed to have involved a horse. On my right sat four Japanese tourists, complete with maps and cameras. In front of them was an American family.

13

Two sullen-faced teenage children looking bored; mother looking hardly any older than her teenage daughter and father looking weary of life, or at least of family life.

I could see Sunderland going redder and redder with growing embarrassment as the head waiter brought him closer and closer to my table. I tried to hide behind what was left of my egg and cress sandwich but it hadn't been very big to start with. 'Ms Reynolds sent her apologies,' the head waiter said to Sunderland. 'She's been unavoidably delayed. She says you know Mr Watson and hopes you won't mind having tea together today.'

Sunderland started to protest. I could see that he was trying to decide whether or not to deny that he knew me. I put down my sandwich, stood up, smiled at him and held out my hand. He took it automatically.

I turned the smile towards the head waiter. 'Thank you!' I grinned inanely. 'That's very thoughtful of Ms Reynolds.'

Sunderland had gone white. He sat down.

A waiter appeared from nowhere and put china and cutlery down in front of him.

'Tea?' I asked. I picked up the tea pot.

He looked at me as if I'd asked him if he'd like to dance. I poured him a cup anyway.

'How did she...,'

'Someone recognised me, put two and two together and got four,' I explained. 'Maybe someone's following you.'

Sunderland looked down at the cup of tea in front of him. Tea seemed to be playing an important part in our relationship.

The waiter returned with a fresh pot of tea and Sunderland and I sat in silence for a few moments. Then I heard someone calling my name. It was a bellboy. His voice seemed loud and clear above the hubbub of tea time conversation. It's a strange thing about the human ear; whatever you're doing you always hear when someone mentions your name. The brain seems to pick out the sound, hone in on it and magnify it. I raised an arm and called the boy over.

He handed me a note. I told Sunderland to tip him. The expenses were getting completely out of hand. The note had a telephone number on it. The prefix told me that the number belonged to a portable phone.

'Wait here,' I said to Sunderland. 'Don't move. Don't do anything. Just drink your tea.'

He looked at me, startled, and opened his mouth.

I never knew whether he finished the question that was on it's way to his mouth because I was already on my way to find a telephone. When I worked for the paper I had a portable telephone too but when I was fired I had to give it back. I missed it; it was a long time since I'd had to use an ordinary public phone box.

The number I dialled was answered on the first ring.

'Sunderland's out of his depth,' I said without waiting for anyone to answer. 'He asked me along to hold his hand. He hasn't been to the police.'

'Good!' said a voice at the other end. A man's voice. 'You can take a message. Tell Sunderland that his wife is safe and well. He'll see her when Jeremy Lonsdale is acquitted.'

I thought I'd misheard. I asked him to repeat what he'd said. He did. I hadn't misheard.

'I don't understand. What's Michael Sunderland got to do with Jeremy Lonsdale?'

'The trial starts next Monday. Ask Sunderland where he's going to be next Monday.'

I still didn't understand but there was something more important to say.

'We want something to prove that Sunderland's wife is alive and well.'

'What?'

'A video or photo of her holding up today's paper. Plus an audio tape of her reading out the headlines. And we want fresh photos and tapes every day that you hold her.'

'O.K. It'll be delivered to Sunderland's flat.'

He put the phone down.

CHAPTER FOUR

I knew of Jeremy Lonsdale, of course. I'd never met him but I'd written about him and I knew that he was about to stand trial for fraud.

When I got back to the table I asked Sunderland how he knew Lonsdale. He looked genuinely puzzled and said that he didn't. I told him what the man on the phone had said and asked him what he was doing the following Monday.

For a moment he looked blank. Then he remembered. It wasn't the sort of thing people usually forget but then Michael Sunderland was under a rather extraordinary amount of pressure.

'I've been called for jury duty,' he said. 'At the Old Bailey.'

It didn't take a great intellect to work it out.

'You're on the jury for the Lonsdale case,' I told him.

He looked puzzled. 'How did you know? I thought they didn't know which jurors were sitting on which juries until the last minute?'

'Just because they don't tell *you* that doesn't mean that no one knows,' I pointed out. 'And Lonsdale certainly knows.'

'Who is Lonsdale?'

'He's the man who's on trial. He's got to be the man who's behind Barbara's kidnapping.'

'What's he done?'

'I don't know what he's done this time but he's been involved in a number of financial frauds over the years. Don't you remember the Trans Continental Casualty Insurance Company?'

Sunderland thought for a moment and then shook his head.

'It made all the papers a few years ago,' I explained. 'It was the first time I heard of him.'

'What did he do?'

'Sold holiday insurance to travellers coming to Britain.'

Sunderland looked puzzled. 'Was there any money in that?'

'Tourism is the world's third biggest industry. About twenty million people a year come to Britain on holiday.'

'And most of them buy travel insurance?'

I nodded. 'At between fifteen and thirty pounds a head.'

Sunderland looked impressed.

'Work it out when you've got a few spare minutes,' I told him. 'A ten per cent share of the business would gross around £40 million a year. And Lonsdale had an edge. He offered travel agents a much bigger commission than any of his rivals – over 50%.'

'How on earth did he manage that?'

'His company offered tourists to Britain private health cover that operated only where they weren't entitled to other, free health cover.'

Sunderland looked puzzled.

'All tourists to Britain are entitled to free health care under the National Health Service,' I explained. 'So Lonsdale's cover didn't cost him anything.'

'But wasn't it illegal?'

'Not really. And as far as I know they never had to pay out a penny. Apart from paying commission to the foreign travel agents – and printing some forms – everything was profit.'

'And what's he done now?'

'I'm going to try and find out,' I told him. 'But this time he must have gone a bit further over the legal boundaries.'

'What have Barbara and I got to do with all this?'

'Simple.' I told him. 'You'll get Barbara back if you find Lonsdale 'not guilty'.'

'But there will be eleven other jurors!' Sunderland protested. 'I can't find him not guilty by myself.'

'Lonsdale knows damned well that on a jury one person invariably influences the result. You're all they need.'

'But why Barbara? Why choose me?'

'You're educated, smart, persuasive. You're a leader. You sell advertising for a living don't you?' I thought it was rather frightening to realise that criminals were now doing psychological profiles of potential jurors.

Sunderland nodded.

'They want you to sell the rest of the jury on Lonsdale's innocence.' I explained.

At that point the waiter brought the bill. I looked at it several times.

'Are you sure this is right?' I pointed to the total.

The waiter looked slightly confused. 'I'm afraid the bill is correct, sir.' he murmured. 'Is there a problem, sir?'

Sunderland reached across the table and took the bill from me. He removed a thin black leather wallet from his inside breast pocket and removed a gold, plastic credit card. He handed the card and the bill to the waiter with a smile.

'I'm sorry,' he said to me. 'I forgot. Peter told me that you'd lost you job. I should pay you something for your help. And cover your expenses.'

'That's all right,' I said, not meaning it. I was just being polite. I didn't think he'd take me seriously. But he did.

'O.K.' he said.

We left The Grand and made our way back to his flat. We took my car which was parked in Jermyn Street. His, which was parked in Piccadilly, had been clamped.

Sunderland and his bride had bought an expensive flat in the Docklands and had furnished it with the sort of furniture that looks good in glossy magazines but is impractical and uncomfortable to use. The flat was on the fifth floor and had a magnificent view of a dusty building site and a dark, oil-stained, sluggish stretch of water.

'What do we do now?' he wanted to know after I'd said 'no' to his offers of American beer, Scottish whisky, French brandy or Italian wine and 'yes' to the offer of a cup of Nicaraguan coffee. I'll drink a glass of champagne at a wedding if I have to but I don't really like alcohol.

'I'm not sure,' I admitted. I tried to find a comfortable position on a chair that had been built out of strips of chromium plated metal and slender strands of plastic. Whichever way I sat the plastic and the chrome sliced into my flesh like a potato chipper slices into a potato.

He sat down opposite me on a chair that looked the twin to the one I'd chosen. He seemed to have forgotten about the offer of coffee. I didn't remind him.

'If I do what they want...,' he began hesitantly, 'do you think they'll...?'

'Will they keep their side of the bargain? Will they let your wife go?'

He nodded.

'No.' There didn't seem any point in lying to him.

'How can you say that with such certainty?'

'Because Lonsdale doesn't like taking risks.' I stood up and walked over to the window. In the distance I could see what looked like a speedboat. For a brief instant I thought it was towing a water skier. 'If he lets your wife go he'll be at risk. He won't like that'

'So, what do we do?'

'I don't know.' The boat was towing a water skier. The skier wore a full body wet suit; presumably to protect him against the oil and the slime and the sewage as much as against the cold.

I heard what sounded like a sob and turned round. Sunderland had his hands over his face and his body was shaking. I felt guilty. I'd been pretty callous about it. I'd forgotten that he probably loved his wife and wanted her back. I turned, walked over to him, bent down and put a hand on his back. But I didn't know what to say.

'I'm sorry...,' he managed to blurt out in between sobs. 'I love her very much.'

'I'll think of something,' I promised him. 'Don't worry.'

He took his hands away from his face and slowly stood up. He looked at me with his eyes full of hope and trust. 'Will you?' He reached out and shook my hand. 'Thank you.' He swallowed noisily. 'Thank you.'

I smiled and winked at him. 'Don't you worry,' I said. 'Everything will be O.K. We'll get your wife back in one piece.'

Most of us make rash promises from time to time.

CHAPTER FIVE

Back in my own flat another wave of depression swept over me and threatened to drown me in its darkness. Looking around I could understand why my wife had packed her bags and left. The flat was cramped and the furniture she'd left was cheap and uninspiring. It was the sort of flat you'd expect a failure to live in. I felt right at home.

After I'd made myself a coffee I decided I'd have a clear out and throw away everything I didn't like or didn't need. I always find something cleansing and cathartic about a spring clean. It helps me to believe that my life is about to start afresh. Maybe I trick myself into believing that together with the old clothes and old papers I can toss out the unwanted emotional baggage and the assorted layers of guilt that I'm so good at collecting.

I did my closet first. That was easy. After twenty minutes I'd filled two black plastic bags with shirts that didn't fit me, trousers that had frayed around the pockets and jackets I didn't like. Half a dozen odd socks went in as did two pairs of black shoes that I'd bought in Rome and that pinched me so badly that I never wore them.

Next I tackled the furniture, daubing a yellow crayon mark on everything I wanted to live the rest of my life without. When I'd finished the flat looked as though it had acquired some unpleasant infectious disease. To make sure I didn't change my mind I picked up the phone and rang a skip hire company. They promised to bring a skip round within the hour. I made them promise to ring the doorbell and let me know when they'd delivered it. Leave an empty skip anywhere in London and it'll be full of other peoples rubbish within minutes. I told myself that anything I didn't like and couldn't afford to replace I'd simply live without. Looking at all the naff furniture I was about to make homeless made me feel closer to feeling content and able to live with myself.

While I waited for the skip rental company to arrive I pulled out a couple of large cardboard boxes that I'd been carrying around with me for years and that I'd kept stuffed under the bed. Both were full of bits and pieces of a past I didn't particularly want reminding about. I emptied both boxes onto the floor so that I could use one for the stuff I was throwing out and the other for the stuff I genuinely couldn't live without.

The junk was unbelievable. Old birthday cards. Pens that didn't work and that no one made refills for any more. My old passport. Old score cards from Lord's cricket ground. Royalty statements from my publishers. A box of typewriter ribbons for a typewriter I'd thrown out years earlier. A smallpox vaccination certificate. Four photocopies of my birth certificate. Old bank statements and receipts. Old diaries. An old address book.

I threw them all into the box for dumping. Then I pulled out the address book. It was full of crossings out and blobs of white correcting ink. Slowly, I turned the pages. Most of the people in it I hadn't seen or spoken to for years. I wondered how many of them were still alive. I wondered if any of them even remembered me. Then I thought how odd it would be if someone in the book just happened to be sorting through his (or her) old rubbish and had just come across an address book with my name and telephone number in it. Then I tossed the old address book back into the box for dumping.

Two minutes later I came across a photograph of a girl I'd been in love with when I was eighteen. She was blonde, beautiful and slender. She wore a yellow and pink bikini and had a pony tail. The photograph was slightly out of focus and the colours had begun to go yellow but she looked unbelievably young, innocent and full of fun.

As I stared at the photograph so I gradually remembered more and more about the girl. I remembered that she had eyes that sparkled and full, soft lips that felt so hot when I kissed them that I thought my mouth was going to burn. I remembered that her name was Jackie and that I hadn't thought about her for twelve, maybe fifteen years. I couldn't remember her last name but I could remember our first date and I could

21

remember the first time we made love and I could remember the fuss her parents made when we said that we wanted to go on holiday around Europe. And I remembered that her name wasn't Jackie it was Lindsay; it was her friend who was called Jackie. And I remembered that she had a tiny birthmark on her left shoulder and that she loved dancing and swimming and that she never worried about her weight or the future or the cost of groceries or what the neighbours thought.

Those were heady, carefree, happy days. There was no hole in the ozone layer and we weren't all living in a greenhouse and people used to swim in the sea without getting diarrhoea and sickness the following day.

Then the doorbell rang and it was the man to tell me that he'd delivered the skip and that if I wanted to use it myself I'd better move fast. I stuffed Lindsay's photograph into my back pocket and spent the rest of the evening carrying furniture down the stairs and throwing it into the skip.

When I started I didn't think I'd be able to get more than a quarter of the stuff I wanted to throw out into the skip but by the time I'd finished people were hauling stuff out of the skip faster than I could put it in. It was like throwing my rubbish into a bottomless black hole. By the time I got to the green Draylon sofa and the matching wing chairs I had no difficulty getting people to help me carry the stuff downstairs.

At ten o'clock, in semi-darkness, I threw the last cardboard box and an orange, plastic pedal bin into the skip and made my way back upstairs.

The only furniture left in the flat was the cooker, the fridge, one table and two chairs, a TV set, an electric fire and a bed. The place looked cold and empty. Or liberated and spacious, depending on which way you looked at it.

I climbed into the bed and went to sleep.

CHAPTER SIX

Jeremy Lonsdale had a country estate near Newbury in Berkshire, an apartment on the Rue de Rivoli in Paris, a chalet in Gstaad in Switzerland, a penthouse flat in Curzon Street in central London and an office in the London nursing home he owned. Since the nursing home was the nearest of these I decided to start there. I was hoping to spot Lonsdale himself. I didn't have a plan.

'We don't do burgers without the burger,' the girl said defiantly, backing away slightly in case I proved dangerous as well as mad.

'I'll pay for the whole thing,' I said wearily, putting money down on the counter. 'But I don't want any meat in it.'

By this time the chef had completed my order. The waitress picked up my small cardboard packet of chips and my ready wrapped burger and threw them down onto a plastic tray.

'If you don't want the meat don't eat it,' she said, sorting out my change. She tossed a few coins onto the tray and then pushed the tray towards me and turned her back. Service twentieth century style.

I thanked her politely, carried my tray to a vacant table and sat down. When I unwrapped the burger the smell of the half raw mixture of gristle, fat and chemical colourants made me nauseous so I rewrapped it and carefully deposited it in a plastic chute. I took my chips outside, walked back towards the nursing home, and ate my spartan lunch in the rain.

By mid-afternoon the rain had eased off and had become nothing more than an irritating drizzle but standing outside Lonsdale's London nursing home remained boring and unproductive.

At four thirty I decided to give up and go back to my own flat which had grown steadily in appeal as the day had progressed. I was tired, wet, cold and hungry and I wanted a bath, a warm meal and a hot drink. I wasn't bothered about the order in which I got them.

*   *   *

An hour later I lay back in the bath, closed my eyes and luxuriated in the comforting warmth of the water. Freud would probably say I've got a womb fixation but I love baths. Showers are all very well for cleaning off the day's dirt but for washing away the day's worries and disappointments you can't beat 18 inches of hot water. A mug half full of sweet tea sat on the soap rack in front of me and I could smell the pan of vegetable hot pot that I'd left simmering on the kitchen stove.

When I had arrived home I'd found two messages on my answering machine. One of them was from Michael Sunderland who'd rung to let me know that when he'd woken that morning he'd found a polaroid of his wife holding the previous day's copy of The Daily Telegraph stuffed in his letter box. There was also an audio tape of her reading out the headlines. Michael said that she looked and sounded nervous but healthy. He wanted to know if I'd made any progress.

The other call was from my wife wanting to let me know that she'd been to visit a lawyer. She said she wanted to marry Jocelyn (the banker) and would I get my lawyer to contact her lawyer so that we could get things sorted out quickly. All the people who'd rung offering me employment or invitations to exotic parties had failed to master the intricacies of leaving a message on my machine.

I spent forty minutes in the bath and then ate my dinner (vegetable hot pot followed by a slab of ice cream dumped into a bowl). By the time I'd washed up (one pan, two dishes and two spoons) it was half past seven. I'd been back in my flat for two hours and I couldn't stand it a minute longer. It wasn't the solitude I didn't like but the flat and the memories it held. Come to think of it I wasn't too keen on the solitude either.

I rang a contact who works for the police on his private line. He was, as I'd hoped, still in his office just preparing to go home.

'Can I buy you a drink?' I asked. I sometimes wonder how the world would go round without alcohol to oil the social wheels. Every deal I've ever been involved in was conceived, planned and confirmed over a drink. Come to think of it every relationship I've ever had (meaningful or not) began with an invitation to meet for a drink. There was a pause before Hutchins spoke. (Hutchins was the name he had given me but I knew it wasn't his real name.) I was surprised. He isn't normally a man to turn down a drink.

'I heard you'd left the paper,' he said at last. 'Got yourself fixed up with another job already?'

Before he'd finished speaking I understood his hesitation. In the world in which he moves an invitation from a journalist to 'have a drink' means an invitation to exchange information for a few ten pound notes, or brown drinking vouchers as they're known.

'I'm freelancing,' I reassured him, thinking that I really would have to have another word with Sunderland. 'Someone's covering my expenses.'

I met him thirty minutes later in a bar in Whitehall.

From the outside you couldn't tell that the bar was there. The entrance, a plain brown door, badly in need of a coat of paint, was marked with a small, official notice telling anyone tall enough, and with good enough eyesight, that Richard Arthur Freenwood was licensed to sell intoxicating liquor. Inside there was a long, functional bar, a dozen bar stools and half a dozen old-fashioned, brass topped tables, each of which was surrounded by three or four old-fashioned wooden chairs.

The pub was frequented by civil servants from the Ministry of Agriculture and Fisheries which had its offices just a few hundred yards away and by policemen from New Scotland Yard which was well within staggering distance. The lack of signs or advertisements outside the pub meant that tourists didn't even know it existed. Even on hot summer days the landlord kept the front door closed to discourage customers from out of town.

I'd ordered a tonic water for myself and a double brandy for Hutchins by the time he arrived.

Hutchins is, I suppose, in his late forties or early fifties and his distaste for personal grooming is so total that whenever I'm with him I always feel well dressed and elegant.

I was wearing a pair of off-white, generously cut corduroy

trousers and a brown leather jacket that I'd had for years. It had been described as 'distressed' leather when I'd bought it but now it was more distressed than ever. I liked it that way. It felt comfortable. It also had a lot of pockets. I love pockets. I had on several occasions wondered about the ethics of a vegetarian wearing a leather jacket but had decided that I couldn't help the cow it had come from by throwing it away and that if I went out and bought a plastic replacement I'd probably be responsible for yet more damage to the environment. So I kept it and wore it.

Hutchins, who is around five foot ten inches tall must weigh at least 15 or 16 stones. He has an enormous paunch which hangs over the top of his trousers and his suits always look cheap and badly cut. The suit he had on that evening was made out of a light grey man-made fibre and bore several stains. A sprinkling of dandruff covered his shoulders. He wore a cream shirt with a narrow, brown polyester tie and the top button of his shirt had been undone and the tie pulled slightly to one side.

'I'm thinking of writing something about Jerry Lonsdale,' I lied. I'd been a journalist for so long that I sometimes worried about the fact that I found it easy to lie. But lying to policemen never worried me, largely because I knew very well that they never told the truth and always assumed that everyone they spoke to was lying too.

'It's all been in the papers already,' said Hutchins, picking up the brandy I'd bought for him without even asking if it was his. I noticed that since I'd seen him last he had deteriorated. He looked seedier than ever. His nose had taken on that purple hue that sometimes affects the heavy drinker and his eyes looked as though they were permanently bloodshot. His hair had thinned a lot more too. He now vainly combed a few strands of thinning ginger hair over his freckled scalp.

'You can't believe what you read in the papers,' I said, sipping at my drink. I didn't want to tell Hutchins that I no longer had ready access to a newspaper cuttings library and I didn't have the time to go to the public library and work my way through all the recent issues of the daily newspapers.

'What do you know?'

'There have been a lot of rumours about him. He's been pulled in a few times but nothing has ever stuck.'

Hutchins tossed the rest of the brandy down his throat and banged the empty glass down on the bar. I started to signal to the barman to refill the glass but he'd beaten me to it.

Hutchins turned to me and leered. 'It's a good story,' he said. 'It'll help you get back on your feet.'

'What do you mean?' I asked him.

He leant on the bar and tilted his head slightly to one side. He hadn't shaved very well and there was a large patch of stubble around his chin. 'Who are you freelancing for?'

'It's on spec.'

'You haven't got anyone lined up, have you?'

'If it's good I won't have any difficulty placing it.'

'But it's going to cost you,' said Hutchins.

'How much?'

'A thousand,' he said. 'I told you, this is a good story.'

He emptied his glass again, winked at me and levered himself up off the bar. 'Ring me if you can get the money,' he said, moving away. 'Cash.'

CHAPTER SEVEN

When I got back to the flat that evening there was another message on my answering machine from Michael Sunderland. He just asked me to ring him back.

'Is there any news?' he wanted to know.

I told him I had a couple of leads but nothing concrete.

There was silence.

'Do you think it would help if I rang the court and told them I wasn't able to turn up for jury duty? I could get a doctor's note.'

I thought about it for a second or two. 'No.'

'Why?'

'Because at the moment we've got a hold over Lonsdale. You're on his jury. If you come off the jury we no longer have a hold over him. And then he doesn't need Barbara.'

'But wouldn't he just let her go?'

'He won't think like that. His first thought will be how it will affect him, not how you or Barbara are feeling. If he lets Barbara go and she talks to the police or the press he'll be in even more trouble than he is at the moment.'

'Isn't there anything I can do?'

'I'm afraid not.'

'What about if I go round to see Lonsdale? I could explain to him that I'll do whatever he wants but that I want Barbara back now – not later.'

'I don't think that's a very good idea.'

'Why not?' Sunderland was getting belligerent now. I guessed that he'd probably been drinking. In his position I'd have wanted to take something to help me forget too.

'Because he doesn't see things logically,' was the best I could manage. I didn't want to tell him that Lonsdale was the sort of man who considered fair play a sign of weakness. For him rules were merely a handicap invented to hinder the opposition. Lonsdale would regard an appeal from Sunderland as simple evidence that he'd chosen the right man to put pressure on. 'I know it's difficult', I said, 'but try to be patient. Just remember that Lonsdale isn't going to hurt you or Barbara while the trial is on. He needs you and he needs Barbara.' I paused. 'There's one other thing,' I added. 'I don't suppose you have a spare grand lying around do you?'

'A grand?'

'A thousand pounds.'

'A thousand! What for?'

'A policeman I know has some information which might be useful. But he wants a thousand pounds for it.'

'Do you think it will help us to find Barbara?'

'I don't know,' I said honestly. 'But it might. It's the best lead I've got.'

'I'll get it,' said Sunderland. 'When do you need it?'

'Whenever.'

'I'll be at your flat by eleven tomorrow morning.'

'He wants cash.'

'O.K.,' said Sunderland. He hesitated. 'And thanks.'
He put the phone down.

I filled the kettle, threw my jacket across the back of one of the chairs in the kitchen and sat down. While the kettle boiled I pulled out the photograph of Lindsay that I'd stuffed into my trouser pocket the night before. I propped the photo up against the salt cellar that stood in the middle of the table and stared at it.

Looking at her reminded me of myself when I was eighteen. Innocent, full of dreams and burning with an urgent desire to change the world. I had read of Van Gogh and dreamt of becoming an artist. I had read a biography of Winston Churchill and dreamt of becoming a statesman, pulling my country from the edge of a terrible abyss through the force of my personality and strength of will alone. I had read Seven Pillars of Wisdom by T.E.Lawrence and dreamt of adventures, alone and far from home. The dreams came back to me suddenly and vividly; as vivid as they had been when I'd first had them.

But what had happened to them?

As I'd grown up I'd been encouraged to set aside my visions

of the future and to replace my thoughts of romance and adventure and selfless simplicity with more personal, more material aspirations.

When I looked at the photograph of sweet and gentle Lindsay I remembered the fantasies of my youth; the ambitions that had been set aside as I had struggled to grow into sensible, prosaic adulthood.

Eighteen seemed a long time ago. The world had changed a million times since then. At least my world had. Innocence had been replaced with cynicism. Youthful hopes had been washed away by waves of scepticism. As I sat there I dreamt of long walks on the beach. I dreamt of nights spent talking not of new hi-fi systems or new dishwashers but of glories, adventures and romances. The dreams and the memories seemed to come from a different world. But it was a world I liked better than the world I was living in now.

I woke feeling cold and stiff. I had fallen asleep with my head resting on my arms and my arms folded on the kitchen table.

It was the telephone that had woken me and as I struggled back to consciousness I heard my answering machine take the call. Dimly, I was aware of my own voice telling the caller that I was out but that if they would leave a message I would get back to them as soon as possible. I struggled to my feet, stretched my sore back and hobbled to the telephone. I turned off the machine and picked up the receiver.

'Hello?' I tried to say. Half my face was still asleep, the muscles numb from the way I'd been sleeping.

'Is that you?' I heard someone say. It was my wife.

'Yes.'

'I thought it was the machine.'

'No.'

'Have you got a lawyer yet?'

'No. I've been busy. What time is it?'

'It's six thirty. You should be up. Jocelyn left the flat two hours ago. He starts work at 5.30 am.'

'I thought he worked in a bank.'

'He's a currency dealer. They never really close. Something to do with the clocks in Tokyo or New York.' She wouldn't care as long as the job brought in lots of money. 'He says you should get yourself a lawyer.'

'I haven't got any money for a lawyer. You go ahead and do what you have to do. I'll sign whatever I have to sign.'

'You should have a lawyer to represent you.'

'What for?'

'You just should.' There was a pause. 'Are you all right? Are you eating properly?'

'I'm all right. But I don't want a lawyer.'

'You should give up that silly vegan stuff. It's very childish.'

'I'm not a vegan. I'm a vegetarian. There's a difference.'

'Whatever. It's not healthy. You sound terrible.'

'Send me the papers and I'll sign them.'

'O.K.,' she sighed. She put the phone down.

I rubbed my cheek and the muscles slowly came back to life. I realised I didn't miss her at all.

Six thirty. Another day to get through.

CHAPTER EIGHT

I parked the Bentley on double yellow lines in Fleet Street and met Terry at a café that used to be patronised by barristers and journalists and is now patronised almost exclusively by barristers. Since the national newspapers had moved out of Fleet Street numerous local bars and cafés had had to struggle to make a living.

I ordered scrambled eggs, mushrooms, tomatoes and toast. Plus a pot of coffee. Terry ordered coffee and toast.

'I don't know how you can eat all that,' he moaned. 'I've got an ulcer,' he told me for the umpteenth time.

He looked like I always thought a man with an ulcer should look like. I've known him for five years and I've never seen him smile. He worries more than anyone else I know. He works as a clerk at the court.

'How do jurors get selected?' I asked him, as he smeared an almost invisible film of butter across his toast. I never feel there's much need to spend too much time on polite preliminaries with Terry.

He looked across at me sharply. 'It's all very confidential,' he said, with a serious shake of his head. 'Very confidential.'

'I don't want to know about the jurors in any particular case,' I assured him. 'Just in general.'

'Well, it's all done by computer now,' he said, slightly disapprovingly.

He nibbled cautiously at the toast. He was nearly six foot tall and must have weighed less than ten stones. I'd only ever seen him in one suit; a dark grey heavy worsted suit that probably cost him a lot when he'd bought it but which must have been good value if you worked out how many hours wear he'd got from it. He was the sort of person who probably knew exactly how many hours wear he'd got out of it. Come to think of it he probably knew how much it had cost him per hour – down to the last fraction of a penny.

'How far ahead does the computer work?' I asked. He always needed prodding. Getting information out of him was like getting milk out of a cow. It needed a knack to get the whole thing started and then constant effort to keep it coming.

'It depends,' he said, carefully wiping a crumb of toast from a corner of his mouth.

'But some time ahead?'

'Well, theoretically, and very confidentially, yes. Names are selected a month – maybe six weeks – ahead.'

'So, purely theoretically, it would be possible to say who the jurors were likely to be in a trial due to start, say, next week?' In fact I knew that Lonsdale must have known the names of the jurors several weeks ago in order for his people to do enough research to find out that Michael Sunderland was the best possibility for blackmail.

'It wouldn't be possible to be that specific,' said Terry, shaking his head. 'It would all be extremely confidential. But the computer would know.' He spoke of the computer with what I now realised was more reverence than anything else. He spoke of it as though it were some sort of God.

'So, if – theoretically speaking, of course – if someone had access to the computer they would be able to find out who the jurors were likely to be on a particular case?'

'But they wouldn't be able to get into the computer!' insisted Terry. 'Access to the computer room is very restricted. It's all highly confidential material.' He nibbled at his toast again then sipped at his milky white coffee.

I wondered how much it would have cost me to get Terry to give me the list of Lonsdale's jurors and slipped a twenty pound note out of my trouser pocket. I reached under the table with it and tapped him on the knee. Terry put down his cup and skilfully removed the note from my grasp. His soft, clammy hand and speed and dexterity reminded me of a trout taking a fly on a still summer evening. I used to fish, though I've given that up too.

'Thanks very much,' I said. I looked at my watch and pushed away my half finished breakfast.

33

'It's a pleasure,' said Terry. 'Always a pleasure to see you.' The note had disappeared. He looked at the remains of the eggs, mushrooms and tomatoes on my plate. 'That's a waste,' he said, disapprovingly. 'A terrible waste.' But he said it like a man who hates waste rather than as a man who has spotted an opportunity to eat up some leftovers.

When I got back to the Bentley there was a traffic warden standing beside it, reading the notices on my windscreen and scratching her head. I smiled at her.

'Thank you,' I said. 'Thanks for looking after the car.' I got in quickly and drove back to the flat before she could harbour any doubts. Two large stickers attached to the Bentley's windscreen save me a small fortune in parking fines. One is an admission ticket to the car park at Buckingham Palace (which I'd acquired when I'd chauffeured a friend attending an evening reception there) and the other, marked simply 'Doctor on Call' is a sticker produced by the British Medical Association for the exclusive use of its members.

* * *

Sunderland was waiting for me on the doorstep of the building where my flat is.

'I'm sorry I'm early,' he said. 'But I've got it. The money.'

'Fine.' I said. I opened the door. 'Let's go in.'

Once inside he took a brown envelope from his inside jacket pocket and held it out to me. It seemed remarkably slim.

'Is that a thousand pounds?'

'In £50 notes. It doesn't seem much does it?'

'There's no guarantee with this,' I told him, taking the envelope. 'No guarantee that the information I can buy will help us find your wife.'

'But you think it will help?'

'At the very least it will help us understand what's going on. And it might give us an edge over Lonsdale.'

I told him about Hutchins and I told him what I'd learned from Terry.

'So Lonsdale got my name from the computer?'

'Easy for him.'

'But don't they guard that sort of information?'

I laughed. 'Once you put information into a computer it's

like publishing it or writing it on the walls. Anyone who really wants it can get it.'

'What happens now?'

I looked at my watch. 'I'm going to try and fix up a meeting with Hutchins for lunchtime. Once I tell him I've got the £1,000 he'll be as keen as I am to meet.'

'Can you trust him?'

'No. But I've paid him for information in the past and he wants to get paid again in the future. He won't lie to me if he thinks I'm going to find out that he's lied.'

'Not even for £1,000?'

I shrugged. 'I hope not,' I said. Sunderland looked worried. 'That's all I can tell you. There aren't any guarantees.'

'Where can we meet after you've seen him?' asked Sunderland.

'Go back to your flat,' I told him. 'I'll ring you.'

'Are you going past a tube station?'

'Yes,' I said. 'Didn't you come in your car?'

Sunderland half smiled and nodded towards my breast pocket and the brown envelope. 'I sold it this morning,' he admitted. He shrugged. For the first time I found myself really liking him.

CHAPTER NINE

Hutchins put a hand in front of his face and tried to suppress a burp. He was making an effort to behave politely because we were, at his insistence, having lunch in a restaurant in Covent Garden that was patronised largely by advertising people. I think he felt it was his sort of place. In truth he was as out of place there as he would have been in any corner of polite society. He'd spent far too long in the police force. Wanting some wine he waved a podgy hand in the direction of the waiter. When the waiter ignored him he clicked his fingers and called 'Garçon!' in a loud voice. Just to make things worse he did it in what he clearly thought was a French accent. With obvious reluctance the waiter minced over and took Hutchins' order for a bottle of claret.

'Lonsdale has always been in the insurance business,' said Hutchins. 'Do you remember the Trans Continental Casualty Insurance Company?'

I nodded.

'He made a fortune out of that but although he's always been pretty good at making money he's always been equally good at losing it – usually on the gaming tables.'

'I'd heard that he's a high roller.'

'One of the highest,' nodded Hutchins. 'Then three years ago he got mixed up with a group of Italians he met in Las Vegas. He's reputed to have lost a fortune at a casino they owned but they ended up bank rolling him and with their money he picked up a controlling share in a small and very nearly defunct company called Universal Life Secure Policy Society.'

'Sounds very impressive.'

Hutchins snorted. 'When he took it over the assets consisted of a six month lease on an office in Wardour Street, a registered address in the city, a couple of typewriters and enough insurance business to pay his cigar bill for a week.'

The wine waiter arrived with a bottle of claret that didn't even have a year marked on the label. Nevertheless Hutchins insisted on studying the label carefully before allowing the waiter to leave the bottle. The wine was one of the most expensive on the list and smelt as though it had been matured in a rusty tanker moored off the East Anglian coast. Hutchins seemed to like it.

'But,' he said, leaning across the table and stabbing a finger in my direction, 'the company had one big asset that Lonsdale liked. It had been founded in 1878 and had at one time earned a Royal crest. Somebody in the Royal Family had probably had his polo ponies insured through it.'

I poured myself a glass of water and sipped at it. I had decided that since no one was getting married I'd avoid the wine. If the smell was anything to go by the wine was probably more suitable for use as paint stripper.

'What was the role of the Italians?'

Hutchins pulled a face. 'Just money men,' he said. He paused. 'They had more money than they knew what to do with. The word was that they were impressed by the fact that Lonsdale was buying into a company that had the right to have a Royal crest on its notepaper but we always felt that there was more to it than that.' He stopped. There was obviously more to come. I raised an eyebrow and waited. 'We think they're involved in a laundering operation,' said Hutchins.

'How?' I knew he didn't mean they were in the clean socks and underpants business.

'Wait a minute,' said Hutchins, holding up a hand, 'I'll come back to that in a minute. First, there's the annuity scam.' He leant forward. 'You'll like this!' he promised me.

The waiter collected our plates. Hutchins had chosen prawns in avocado. I'd had a tomato salad. The menu had promised that the tomatoes had been 'sun dried in Florida'. Why would anyone care? Wherever they were dried they tasted of nothing at all.

'Some time ago Lonsdale decided to get into the annuity business,' Hutchins continued. He suddenly leant across the table until his face was about a foot from mine. 'Are you sure you've got the cash?' His breath smelt of brandy as well as wine, even though it was still only lunchtime.

I patted my breast pocket and smiled at him. 'It's all here.'

'Cash?'

'Cash.'

He seemed comforted by this. 'Do you know how the annuity business works?'

I thought for a moment. 'Not really.'

'Well the idea is very simple. Old wrinklies who've got a few quid but who are worried about making sure that they have enough income to live on for the rest of their lives sign over all their assets to the insurance company in return for a fixed, annual income.'

'And when they die the insurance company owns the assets?'

'You've got it. It's ideal for wrinklies who don't have any relatives to leave their money to or who don't care a fig about the relatives they've got.'

The waiter brought one T bone steak and one mushroom stroganoff.

Hutchins dug his knife into his steak. Blood oozed out onto the plate. He grinned and cut off a chunk. The waiter returned with the potatoes and the vegetables.

'Lonsdale decided that this was the business to be in,' said Hutchins when the waiter had disappeared again. 'He realised that the number of wrinklies is growing faster than anything else and that they're all terrified of being poor in their old age. To make sure that he got their money he offered the richest – and the loneliest – of them annuities at fantastic rates of up to 20% or 25%.'

I whistled through my teeth and pushed the mushroom stroganoff to one side. The mushrooms were cultivated and had about as much taste as the tomatoes. 'How could he make a profit?'

Hutchins chewed at his steak. 'We think he's got an edge that means he can't lose.'

I nibbled on a stale bread roll and waited for Hutchins to go on.

'Somewhere along the line Lonsdale had also come across a company that runs a chain of private hospitals and nursing homes all over Europe. Dozens of the bloody things. All full of rich wrinklies.' Hutchins reached for the ketchup bottle and poured a large dollop onto the side of his plate. The ketchup and the puddle of blood merged into one another.

'Lonsdale liked the nursing home business for two reasons,' said Hutchins. 'First, it gave him direct access to a mass of old people to whom he could sell his annuity policies. And second it gave his friends from Las Vegas a chance to increase the size and scope of their business.'

'How?'

'No nursing home ever becomes fully occupied,' said Hutchins. 'But Lonsdale's group hasn't had a spare bed since it's been opened.'

'Fake patients?'

'Exactly! They set up fake files for non existent patients and they have a perfect route for laundering vast quantities of money – regularly.'

'What's the name of the company?'

Hutchins tapped the side of his nose and winked at me.

'I'm paying you for all this!' I reminded him. 'I'm going to have to check everything out. I need names.'

Hutchins stared at me for a moment and then shrugged. 'O.K.' he said at last. He spelt out the name for me as he cut off another huge chunk of steak. Then he pierced the steak with his fork and pushed it into his mouth. I waited while he chewed at it.

'The boss of the nursing home chain is a doctor called Simpson who's about as greedy as Lonsdale,' said Hutchins. 'We think that he and Lonsdale have come up with a scheme that means that they can't lose even when Lonsdale is paying out 20–25% on the annuities.'

I put down the bread roll I'd been nibbling. The sight of Hutchins eating was enough to make anyone anorexic. He mopped up the mixture of ketchup and blood with his bread roll and then used his napkin to wipe his face. He belched loudly and contentedly. 'We think they're making sure that the really rich people who buy annuities don't live too long,' he said.

I stared at him. 'How?'

Hutchins shrugged. 'God knows.' He called the waiter over again and asked for the menu. 'Whatever it is Simpson is probably behind it. He's medical director of the whole group of nursing homes.'

When the menu came Hutchins ordered a double peach melba with cream. I ordered some brie and another roll. We both ordered coffee.

I didn't like Hutchins. He wasn't a likeable man. But I was beginning to feel a certain sympathy for him. He perhaps wasn't quite as stupid or as bad a policeman as I'd thought him to be.

'So, what's Lonsdale in court for?'

'We've been after them both for months,' sighed Hutchins. 'We haven't been able to get Simpson for anything. But we've got Lonsdale in court on some technicalities. It's minor league stuff but if we can get a conviction we should be able to get him put away for a few years. It might slow him down a bit, at least.'

The waiter brought Hutchins his double peach melba and me my bread and cheese. The second bread roll was as stale as the first and the brie was nowhere near ripe. It cut like cheddar. I pushed the bread and the cheese to one side and watched Hutchins spoon up his pudding.

'Good meal that, wasn't it?' he said, wiping his mouth again. 'Always get a good meal here. Get what you pay for in this world, don't you?'

I smiled thinly.

'Shall we have some brandy?'

'Not for me. But you have one.'

Hutchins ordered himself a double brandy.

I pushed my chair back and stood up. I reached into my jacket pocket and pulled out the brown envelope that Sunderland had handed me a couple of hours earlier. I suddenly realised that I hadn't even counted it. I put the envelope down in front of Hutchins.

'Thanks!' I said. 'I'm sorry to leave you but I have to go.

'Not staying for coffee?' Hutchins weighed the envelope in one hand and then quickly stuffed it into his jacket pocket. He didn't count it either. Maybe he would pass it on to a bookie who'd pass it on to a punter and no one would ever count it. I turned away and walked quickly to the nearest door before Hutchins realised that I'd left him to pay for the meal.

CHAPTER TEN

I had learned a lot about Lonsdale. But I was no closer to helping Barbara Sunderland. I left the Bentley parked where it was and walked from the restaurant to the National Writers' Club in Whitehall where I'd agreed to meet Sunderland.

The National Writers' Club is a splendid nineteenth century gentleman's club that is, like all its London contemporaries, struggling to survive in the hope that the twenty-first century will bring more prosperity than the twentieth century has brought. I've been a member for years but hardly ever use the club. The best thing about it is that hardly anyone else seems to use it either and so it's a good place to have quiet meetings.

Sunderland was waiting for me in the lobby. I led him up the impressive marble staircase to the smoking room on the first floor. The room was deserted. We settled ourselves in soft leather armchairs and I called the elderly porter over to order buttered toast and tea for two.

'I thought you'd just had lunch?' said Sunderland, surprised.

'Hutchins ate, I watched,' I explained. I told him what I'd learned.

'Nothing about Barbara?' he said. He looked disappointed.

'Not directly,' I admitted. 'But it helps.'

The porter arrived, carrying a large silver tray upon which were crammed: a huge dish of buttered toast, two side plates, two huge silver knives, a pot of marmalade, a pot of gentleman's relish and a pot of strawberry jam, a huge silver tea pot, a silver water jug, a jug of milk, two cups, two saucers and two crested spoons. The porter put the tray down on a low wooden table and withdrew slowly. He had something wrong with his right leg and his hearing aid whistled occasionally. He'd forgotten the sugar but I didn't like to mention it.

41

'So, what do we do now?' Sunderland wanted to know.

I wished he didn't always seem to expect me to know all the answers. I was thrashing around almost as much as he was. The only real difference was that he loved Barbara and I hardly knew her. That just about gave me the edge on objectivity and clarity of thought.

Sunderland didn't wait for me to reply. 'You realise that I'll still help him go free, don't you?' he said suddenly and defiantly. 'Even knowing what you've just told me?'

I looked at him and nodded. 'I wouldn't expect you to do anything else,' I told him. 'In your position I'd do the same.' But I knew I'd feel bad about it and I knew he did.

We sat in silence and watched the butter melting into the toast. Eventually I poured us both cups of steaming hot tea and took a slice of toast. The silver tea pot dribbled badly and a puddle of hot tea appeared on top of the table.

'There's one thing I still don't understand,' said Sunderland thoughtfully. 'Why did Lonsdale arrange for Barbara to be kidnapped in Paris? Why not wait until we got back to London?'

'Makes it more difficult for you, I suppose. If she'd disappeared in London you'd have been able to go straight to the police and they'd have probably taken you more seriously. In France...on holiday...,' I shrugged. 'It was probably just as easy for Lonsdale to kidnap her there as it would have been in London.'

'Do you think she's still over there? Or do you think he's brought her back to England?'

'God knows. I suppose he could just as easily rent a house in France as in England. It would probably be safer keeping her in France. It would save taking her through customs and it would mean that the crime had only been committed in one country.'

I noticed that Sunderland was holding out an envelope. I'd missed what he said. I asked him to repeat it.

'I've been thinking about things and I want you to have this,' he said. He put the envelope down on the table in front of me.

'What is it?'

'Another thousand. But this time it's for you.'

'What the hell for?'

'Expenses. Stuff like that.'

I looked at it. I needed the money but didn't like taking it.

'It's more of the money I got for the car,' explained Sunderland. 'I'm very grateful for what you're doing but it isn't right for you to keep on spending your own money.'

I hesitated.

'Really,' said Sunderland. 'I've got some cash now. I want to pay you five hundred a week for as long as it takes. I really need you.'

'O.K.,' I said. 'Thanks.' I put the envelope into my breast pocket.

CHAPTER ELEVEN

Michael Sunderland took a taxi back to his flat and I started to walk back to the car. On the way I stopped at a telephone box and rang an acquaintance who works as city editor on one of the Sunday newspapers. He owes me more than a few favours.

'I'm sorry,' said the girl who answered the phone. 'Mr Gillespie is tied up in conference.'

'How long will he be?' I resisted the temptation to make any cracks about his sado-masochistic tendencies.

'An hour at least. We're holding all his calls. If you leave your number I'm sure he'll get back to you.' The girl sounded as if she was chewing gum and her voice had a distant, disinterested quality which suggested that she was busy doing something else. I gave her my home number and the number of the gym and then I put the phone down. For some inexplicable reason I felt better than I had for days. I felt better than I had since my wife had left me. Maybe there was life despite divorce and unemployment after all. I think that having Sunderland's money in my pocket helped. But I think that knowing that someone needed me helped even more.

* * *

I went to the gym and worked on the speed ball for fifteen minutes then worked up a sweat on the heavy bag. I did five sets of reps on every machine I could find and finished off with a fifteen minute fast session with the rope. I was, inevitably, in the shower again when Billy called me to the telephone.

It was the city editor I'd contacted earlier.

'How are you? I hear you left Patterson's mob.'

Patterson was my former editor. 'Yeah. They said they wanted to give me an opportunity to explore my capabilities.'

'Get a nice pay off'?

I didn't understand what he meant. I said so.

'Redundancy. You've been there a few years haven't you?'

'Yes.' Amazingly I'd never thought about redundancy money. No one had mentioned it to me and I hadn't thought to ask.

'It should go through automatically,' he assured me.

'How do you know so much about it?'

'I've been given opportunities to explore my capabilities at least three times.' He half put his hand over the phone and I heard him shouting to someone about a news story he wanted. Then he was back. 'What can I do for you? I don't suppose you rang me for personal financial advice.' He sounded pushed. In the background I could hear someone shouting.

I mentioned the name of the nursing home group that Hutchins had given me. 'What do you know about it?'

'Run by a greaseball called Simpson. There's rumoured to be some sort of tie up with that scheming little rat what's his name...,'

'Lonsdale.'

'That's him. What do you want to know?'

'Anything you've got.'

'It's all in the computer. I can run you off a print out.'

'Thanks. That would be great. Will it have a list of all the addresses of the hospitals and nursing homes they run?' I shivered and pulled my towel tighter.

'Probably not.'

'O.K. Never mind. I'll take what you've got.'

'You owe me.'

'I owe you? Put this on account!'

He laughed. 'Do you want to pick it up?'

'Yes please.'

'Do you mind if I leave it at the reception desk for you? We're a bit tied up at the moment.'

'That's fine.'

He paused. 'There isn't anything here that I should know about? There isn't a story you should be giving me?'

'No.' I said and put the telephone down.

I finished my shower, dried, dressed and picked up the print out on the way back from the gym. Then I drove straight back to my flat.

The computer had stored every imaginable detail about the company's financial strengths and weaknesses (at least those of them that Simpson and Lonsdale wanted to share with the world) but, as I'd been warned, the print out contained no details of the whereabouts or addresses of the company's physical assets: its hospitals and nursing homes. There was, however, a telephone number for the company's Director of Public Affairs. I rang the number. An answering machine told me that the office was closed but that if I called back another time any routine queries would be attended to without any further delay. The disembodied voice then gave me a phone number to call in emergencies.

I dialled the emergency telephone number that I'd copied down from the answering machine.

'Hello?' The woman who answered sounded harassed and impatient.

I told her my name and explained that I was a journalist working to a deadline. I'd never been more serious about the deadline.

'I'll help you if I can,' she said. She sounded as though it was all an effort for her.

'I just need a list of all the hospitals and nursing homes run by the company.'

'May I ask what for?'

'I'm preparing a feature on private medicine.' I lied.

'Have you got a fax machine?'

'Yes.'

'I'll fax you the list. Give me your fax number.'

Minutes later I was staring at a four foot long list of addresses and telephone numbers.

CHAPTER TWELVE

The photograph of Lindsay was still propped up against the salt cellar where I'd left it. Each time I looked at her she seemed prettier. She was fresh and full of life and there was a beguiling innocence in her eyes that I found irresistible. Had I really once been that innocent? I could remember parties we had been to, music we'd shared and friends we'd had fun with. I could remember the first rock concert we'd been to together, the picnics we'd had and our first kiss. Was life really so much purer and simpler then?

I wondered what had happened to her. Where was she living? Was she married?

I was half way through dialling her number when I stopped and slammed the phone down. My heart was beating as though it was trying to escape from my chest.

It hadn't taken me long to get her number. Two calls to old school friends had been enough. The second person I called told me that she was divorced and had reverted back to her maiden name. They gave me her phone number. She was, apparently, working in television.

I picked up the phone and dialled again. This time I managed to get to the end without putting the receiver down.

Lindsay answered on the fifth ring. I recognised her voice instantly. She sounded as fresh and as lively and as innocent as ever.

I didn't know what to say and could only wonder why I hadn't prepared something witty and bright.

'Hello!' I managed, 'You might not remember me. Mark Watson.' Gauche. Unoriginal. Guarded. Negative.

There was a long pause and then she laughed. Her laugh was every bit as beautiful as I remembered it.

'I hope it isn't a bad time to call.' More negativity. Giving her an excuse to put the phone down. Giving myself an excuse for rejection.

'No, no!' she said quickly. 'What on earth made you call? It's wonderful to hear from you.' Her voice had hardly changed at all.

'I found some old photographs,' I said. 'I thought I'd just give you a ring. See how you are.'

'Can we meet?'

'Yes. I'd like that very much.' There was a pause. I felt as clumsy as a teenager trying to arrange his first date.

'How lovely to hear from you!' She laughed again. Bubbly. Uncomplicated. Bright. Or was she nervous too? 'Where are you?'

I told her. I suddenly remembered an open-topped, frog-eyed Sprite I'd once owned. And a picnic by the Thames. Hot sun, fresh bread and cheese. Making love afterwards on an old car rug in the long grass.

'I know it. You're not far away. Let's meet for dinner. Do you know La Coupole on the Old Brompton Road?'

I said I didn't but assured her that I could find it and arranged to meet her there in an hour. I showered, shaved and put on the one clean shirt I had left. White cotton with a button down collar. Then the suit. Steel grey Yves St Laurent with broad lapels and as almost invisible pale red stripe. Red silk tie with a small, dark grey boxed pattern. Black brogues.

I'd bought the suit at my wife's insistence four years ago. I'd been plumper and out of condition then. It felt tight across the shoulders and the trousers were a little loose around the waist. I found a black leather belt in a drawer.

When I got to the restaurant my heart was going through its escape routine again. This really was like being a teenager on a first date. I found a parking space a few hundred yards from the restaurant and went straight in.

A spindly youth in an evening suit and an elasticated bow tie came over to me, rubbing his hands together as though trying to wash away some nasty social stains. He raised a manicured eyebrow.

'I'm meeting someone,' I said. I peered over his shoulder into the gloom but could see no one I recognised. I suddenly realised that I was looking for someone aged 18 and wearing a pink gingham frock with a lace collar. 'Miss Lindsay Morrison,' I told him.

'Ah, Ms Morrison,' said the spindly youth. He emphasised the 'Ms' so that it sounded as though there was a 'z' in it. 'She did telephone to reserve a table but she isn't here yet.' He looked me up and down and smiled superciliously. 'Would you like a drink while you wait?' He waved an arm in the direction of a small bar area. A couple wearing evening dress were sitting on the only bench seat with their arms around each other. The four bar stools were all vacant.

I was feeling rather dangerous and reckless so I ordered an Indian tonic water with ice and a slice of lemon. The barman, a youth of about twenty wearing a red blazer, brought me a luke warm bottle of tonic water and a stemmed wine glass. There was a quarter of a slice of lemon lying in the bottom of the glass.

'Meeting someone?'

I nodded.

'Want to order another drink?'

'Not yet thanks.' I didn't know what to order. I doubted if she still drank Babycham.

'Suit yourself.'

I took a few notes out of my left hand trouser pocket. 'What do I owe you?'

He told me. It was just slightly more than the price of a good bottle of supermarket wine. I paid him.

I thought I perhaps wouldn't recognise her but I needn't have worried. She came straight over to the bar when she arrived. However much we may think we alter over the years our eyes never really change.

'I'm sorry I'm late. My phone wouldn't stop ringing. I got to the door three times. You know what it's like!'

She seemed taller than I remembered. But she was wearing high heels. Her hair was cut short and it framed her face. The eyes were still as captivating. As were the long eyelashes. And the beautiful, kissable lips. And the perfect teeth. She was wearing a bottle green silk dress that showed off her figure to perfection.

She put one hand on my shoulder and kissed me on the cheek.

'What are you doing these days? Didn't I see your by-line in one of the papers? Where are you living? Isn't this a wonderful surprise?'

I started to ask if she wanted a drink and noticed too late that the barman had already poured and handed her a vodka on ice.

'You look wonderful!' she said. She smiled her thanks to the barman and took a long sip from her drink. She had a thin gold necklace round her neck and wore simple gold earrings. Her eyes were brighter and even more full of life than I remembered.

The spindly youth in the elasticated bow tie materialised. He was holding two large menus. 'Your table is ready, Ms Morrison.' He handed Lindsay one of the menus and gave me the other.

On our way to the table Lindsay said 'hello' to half a dozen diners. She seemed well known. Twice she stopped to kiss people and to introduce me.

'The bass is wonderful here this week,' she confided, after we'd sat down.

I smiled thinly. 'I don't eat fish.' I apologised.

'Then the lamb. With a bottle of the St Emilion.'

'I'm vegetarian.'

She laughed out loud. The people at nearby tables looked across towards us. It was the laugh I remembered best. I didn't know why but I suddenly felt a twinge of pain.

'You didn't used to be a vegetarian!' she reminded me needlessly.

'No,' I agreed. I studied the menu. I couldn't see anything I could eat.

The spindly youth, who'd been hovering, moved forwards to take our orders. Lindsay ordered a green salad followed by the bass. I ordered a melon and a plateful of vegetables.

The spindly youth waited, silver pencil poised.

'And a bottle of St Emilion.' I said.

'And with your vegetables, sir?'

'Just the vegetables, thank you.'

He looked distressed. 'I'm not sure that we can.'

'I'll pay for the lamb,' I said. 'But I don't want it.'

'How long have you been a vegetarian?' asked Lindsay, when he'd gone.

'A few years.' I pulled the quarter of a slice of lemon out of my empty tonic water glass and nibbled at it. 'What are you doing now?'

'Apart from the programme, you mean?'

'What programme is that?'

She blushed. 'I've been producing an arts programme for the BBC,' she told me. 'The last series has just finished.'

I pulled a piece of lemon peel out of the gap between my front teeth.

'Things are a bit quiet at the moment,' she went on. 'But I'm hoping to start work on a two part special for Christmas next month. And there's talk of a thirteen part series for next year on Russian culture.'

'Sounds great,' I said. 'I don't get a chance to watch much television,' I apologised. It had been too long since I'd seen her and with sadness I realised that we now seemed to have only the past in common. I didn't want it to be that way.

A youth in a white jacket brought Lindsay's salad and my melon.

'It sounds a very exciting job,' I said. Someone had spent hours turning my melon into small pink balls. I hate it when people mess with my food.

'Yes,' said Lindsay. She toyed with her salad. 'Very hectic and demanding but very rewarding.'

'Wonderful!' I said. I put one of the pink melon balls into my mouth. It tasted of something odd. It took me a moment to realise that it was Angostura bitters.

An hour and a half later I offered to drive Lindsay home but she said she would arrange for a car to pick her up. She explained that the television company gave her free access to a car hire company.

'It's so much easier than trying to park a car in London.' She hesitated and then leant towards me and kissed me on the cheek again. 'It's been wonderful to see you.' She smiled, reached out and touched me briefly on the arm. I wanted to hold her tight, to hug her, to try to recapture the past, but I didn't dare. 'You haven't changed a bit!' she said. I didn't know whether that was a compliment or not.

I left her sitting at the bar talking to a crowd of friends and waiting for her car to arrive. She asked me to stay but she seemed to belong to a different world. I walked back to the

Bentley feeling a deep sense of sadness and isolation. Now even my memories were disappearing. I didn't know what I'd expected but I wished I hadn't telephoned her. It had been a foolish thing to do.

CHAPTER THIRTEEN

'You were right,' said Sunderland. 'They did know which jury I was going to be on.'

'Lonsdale?'

He nodded.

I sipped at the orange juice he'd poured me. It was out of a tin and the additives and flavourings successfully masked the taste of the oranges.

'What happened today?'

'Nothing much. It was all preliminary stuff. ' There was a pause. 'I saw him for the first time. He seems an arrogant bastard. Very confident.'

'You'd look confident if you knew that you'd nobbled the jury.'

Michael Sunderland looked at me sharply. 'I don't like that word.'

'What word?'

'Nobbled.'

I didn't say anything.

'That's not fair.'

'I'm sorry,' I said. 'How would you describe it?'

He started to cry.

I turned away and looked out of the windows again. There was no sign of the water skier. Part of me wanted to go across to Sunderland, put an arm around him and tell that everything was going to be all right. But I didn't know whether I had the strength he needed. I felt depressed, lonely and tired. And I couldn't see how we were going to be able to get his wife back in one piece.

Behind me I could hear that he was trying to stifle his sobs. It was worse than if he'd just cried. I turned back, walked over to him and put my arms around him. He tensed for a moment and then he suddenly relaxed. His body shook as he cried his heart out. I held onto him and strangely felt his need and his dependence giving me strength.

A few moments later he slowly pushed himself away.

'I'm sorry,' he said. He pulled a freshly laundered handkerchief out of his breast pocket and blew his nose loudly. Then he wiped his eyes.

'You're right,' he said. 'I've been nobbled.'

'Of course you haven't. It was a stupid thing to say.'

'I've been nobbled,' he insisted. 'I don't care what evidence they produce in court I'll find Lonsdale not guilty. All I care about is getting Barbara back safely.'

'I'd be the same,' I said. 'So would anyone. Have you heard from them today?'

For a moment he looked puzzled.

'From the people who've taken Barbara. They're supposed to send you a photograph and a tape recording every day to show that she's all right.'

Michael nodded. He crossed the room and picked a large brown padded envelope off the top of a bookcase. He handed it to me. Inside was a cassette tape and a photograph of Barbara holding up a copy of yesterday's Daily Telegraph. Michael took the cassette tape and slipped it into a tape player. We listened to Barbara's shaky voice reading out one of the stories from the previous day's front page.

'How long will she be safe?' Michael asked me.

I was studying the photograph. Barbara was standing but the background was blurred.

'They won't do anything to hurt her while the trial is on,' I said. I held up the photograph. 'Can I borrow this? I want to get it enlarged.'

Michael nodded. 'Of course.'

I left the cassette tape in the player and put the photograph back into the padded envelope.

CHAPTER FOURTEEN

When I left Michael Sunderland's flat I headed for the Daily Telegraph's offices. They were less than a mile away.

First, I spoke to a guy on the picture desk, whom I'd known for years. I asked him to get the photograph of Barbara enlarged as much as possible.

Then, while I waited for the laboratory to come up with the print I wanted, I went to the advertising department and asked them to let me look at the previous day's editions of the paper.

The edition that Barbara had been holding up was the very first, earliest edition.

'Where does this edition go?' I asked the girl who'd found me the various copies of the paper.

'The West Country mainly,' she replied.

'What about the North of England?'

'They get an edition that's printed in Manchester.'

Thirty minutes later my friend from the picture desk turned up with the enlarged photograph of Barbara. 'Who's this?' he demanded. 'What's the point in having a blow up of a bird holding a copy of the Telegraph?'

'It's just a bit of a joke for a friend,' I said.

He shook his head, muttered something rude and disappeared.

Back in my flat I pinned Barbara's enlarged photograph on the kitchen wall. Then I held up the previous day's first edition of the Daily Telegraph at the side of the photograph. I stared at them both in turn.

The edition Barbara was holding was quite definitely the first edition. But there was something different about it. I just couldn't decide what it was.

I went into my bedroom and dug out the list of nursing

homes that had been faxed through to me. There were two in the West Country. One in Plymouth and the other in Exeter.

Maybe Barbara was being held in one of those.

I went back into the kitchen and stared at Barbara's picture again. And then I spotted the difference between the edition that Barbara was holding and the edition that I had laid out on my kitchen table.

In the Stop Press section that I was holding there were two small pieces of late sporting news. One about a football match and the other about a golf tournament. But the Stop Press section of the paper that Barbara was holding carried neither of these news items. Instead it contained what was clearly a list.

I moved right up to the photograph and stared at it. I couldn't quite decipher what was on the list.

I raced back into the bedroom. There was nothing there that would help. I pulled open the drawers in all the kitchen cupboards. Nothing.

Desperate now I raced downstairs and out into the street. I needed a toy shop. Why is there never a toy shop around when you need one?

I ran along the street trying to remember where I'd seen a toy shop. Every building I passed seemed to be a building society or an estate agency.

When at last I found one and told the counter assistant what I wanted he shook his head as though I'd asked for a pound of wet fish.

'You must have one!' I insisted.

He shook his head and turned away.

Suddenly I had a flash of inspiration. 'A detective set! You must have a detective set!'

'Of course!' he said, wearily. 'If that's what you wanted why didn't you say so?' He disappeared and returned a few moments later with a huge cardboard box on the front of which was a rather bad drawing of Sherlock Holmes set against an equally poor drawing of Victorian London.

I paid him the exorbitant price on the lid and impatiently opened the box. There was a small plastic pipe, a notebook, a pencil, a cheap deerstalker hat, a plastic revolver. And a magnifying glass.

Taking the magnifying glass and leaving the rest I rushed out of the shop and raced back to my flat.

The magnifying glass was just strong enough for me to read what appeared in the Stop Press section of the newspaper that Barbara was holding. It was a list of foreign currency prices for the Daily Telegraph abroad. The early editions – the ones that go to the West Country – also go to the airport for distribution abroad.

Excitedly, I moved my magnifying glass up to the top right corner of the newspaper – the spot where newsagents invariably write on the price of the paper they're selling so that tourists can easily see it. I could just read the scribbled price. It matched the price in French francs that was listed in the Stop Press section.

Barbara was still in France – somewhere that English papers were on sale.

I raced into my bedroom and found the faxed list of nursing homes owned by Lonsdale and Dr Simpson.

There was one in Paris.

It was all so obvious I couldn't believe that I hadn't thought of it before. I rang the airport straight away and spoke to the girl at the reservations desk.

CHAPTER FIFTEEN

The nursing home had been converted from a large house that stood in wooded grounds on the Eastern side of Paris. I walked through the huge, imposing gates and along the driveway towards a gothic building that had been carefully and sympathetically restored to all its former glory. The lawns and flower beds were immaculate. Neat pink and white awnings shaded every window.

The main hall of the house had been converted into a reception area. Straight ahead of me there were half a dozen huge red leather armchairs neatly lined up behind a low, glass topped coffee table upon which were strewn a number of expensive magazines. To the left, behind a huge, antique wooden desk, sat a blonde receptionist. She wore a simple blue dress upon which was pinned a white enamel badge which told the world that her name was Elaine. She took her job seriously. She was neither reading a paperback romance nor painting her finger nails.

She smiled and showed me two rows of neatly and expensively capped teeth. 'Can I help you?'

I leant across the desk and smiled back. I couldn't match the capped teeth. 'I'm looking for somewhere suitable for my mother,' I lied. 'She's elderly and can't cope at home any more. My company has moved me to Paris and I'm looking for somewhere for my mother to stay – somewhere permanent.'

'Certainly!' said the receptionist. She didn't stop smiling. 'If you'd be kind enough to take a seat for a few moments I'll ask Monsieur Heraud, our General Administrator, to have a word with you.' She waved one immaculately manicured hand towards the leather arm chairs and with the other hand picked up a pale blue telephone.

The General Administrator must have been hiding behind

the oak panelling that lined the reception area. He appeared soundlessly and without warning just a few seconds later. He was wearing an expensive, hand made pinstripe three piece suit, a white silk shirt, grey silk tie, fixed with a gold pin, and black shoes that sparkled.

'Shall we walk while we talk?' His dental work made the receptionist look as though she needed an urgent appointment for remedial work. 'I can explain a few things to you and answer any questions you may have and you can see how well your mother will be looked after here.'

I followed him down a broad corridor. His shoes made a sharp clicking sound on the exquisite mosaic floors.

'This is one of our typical rooms,' he said, opening a door apparently at random and ushering me into a spacious and well-appointed room which contained a large bed, two easy chairs, a writing desk and chair and a television set. He opened two more doors, one of which led into a spacious, walk-in closet and the other which led into a large, marble-floored bathroom. 'All our nursing staff are fully trained,' he confided.

'It's very impressive,' I nodded. It was. I guessed that the bills would be pretty impressive too.

The tour of the hospital took fifteen minutes. I saw the two operating theatres, the intensive care unit, the recreation rooms, the private cinema and the heated swimming pool. It seemed to be a combination of hospital and luxury hotel. Someone had spent a lot of money on it.

'There is one other room I'd like you to see,' said Heraud. He took what looked like a plastic credit card from a wafer-thin wallet and inserted it into a slit in a small metal panel by the side of a door that had no door handle. An electric motor whirred and the door slid sideways into a cavity in the wall.

I followed him into a room about twenty feet square. There were single large windows in two walls and the wall on our left had a door in it which led into the room I could see through the windows.

'That is our computer room,' said Heraud proudly, pointing through the glass. 'I'm afraid I can't take you into the room itself because we follow very strict security and have to follow precise rules to avoid any dust contamination.' I followed him until we were both standing close to one of the windows. The room on the other side of the glass contained a complex assortment of sophisticated computer equipment. Several figures in white coats, white trousers, white hats and white plastic overshoes were sitting at desks.

'We use these computer files for everything we do,' said Heraud. 'We have forty nursing homes – spread throughout most European countries – but all our patients' records and our financial affairs are coordinated here. Each one of our nursing homes has a subsidiary computer room which enables them to feed us with information and enables us to pass on instructions from Dr Simpson, our Group Medical Director in London.'

'My mother doesn't like computers very much,' I said rather hesitantly. 'She's very nervous about them.'

'Good heavens!' said Heraud, obviously startled. 'Why on earth is that?'

'Confidentiality,' I said simply. 'She doesn't trust them.'

Heraud put a hand on my arm. 'Your mother has absolutely nothing to worry about here,' he promised me. 'All the information stored here is extremely confidential and can only be reached by using special code words. Staff members only have access to information that they need to do their jobs properly.' He frowned. 'We take confidentiality very seriously.'

One of the white-coated men took a reel of computer tape from one machine and replaced it with another reel.

'Many of our clients allow us to manage their financial affairs for them and our investment experts have direct access to banks and financial markets through our computer,' said Heraud. 'They have absolute faith in it's safety and confidentiality. Our chairman, Mr Lonsdale, and our group medical director, Dr Simpson, both work from London and have computer terminals but they have very personal, confidential methods of getting access to the stored information.' He leant a little closer. 'Passwords!' he whispered.

'And you use the computer to store the medical records of all your patients?'

'We certainly do,' nodded Heraud proudly. 'We don't use paper records at all. Every nursing station and every room in each of our nursing homes has its own keying in procedure so that nurses can use the system for consulting or recording confidential information about our residents. Our doctors even use our computers to record drug therapies – they find it reduces the risk of errors. There is a computer monitor by the side of every resident's bed so that our doctors and nurses can call up whatever information they need. Our laboratories and X ray units feed the results of their investigations and tests directly into the computer system so that there are no delays.'

One of the white-coated computer operators turned round, saw us and smiled. A fringe of jet black hair peeped out from underneath her white hat. She waved. I waved back. Heraud wasn't the sort of person who ever waved. 'We have enough computer capacity here to keep confidential individual medical records on hundreds of thousands of patients,' he told me proudly.

From the anteroom to the computer centre Monsieur Heraud ushered me back along a corridor and into his office, a magnificent room with views across the lawns. A huge chandelier hung from a ceiling that must have been thirty foot high and the walls were lined with glass-fronted bookcases, all filled with leather-bound volumes.

Gingerly, I sat down on what I guessed was a valuable antique chair while Heraud picked up his telephone and asked someone to bring in tea for two. He then handed me a large, glossy brochure.

'Do you have any questions?' he asked.

'It's all very impressive,' I said. I flicked through the brochure and pulled out a loose price list. I studied it carefully. The rooms were slightly more expensive than rooms at The Ritz in the Place Vendôme in the centre of Paris.

'My mother has her own house which we are planning to sell for her,' I said. 'She'll then have a fairly large sum of money which we will want to invest on her behalf.'

Heraud looked interested the way a dog looks interested when it sees a bone but he simply nodded sternly. Money clearly wasn't a subject for smiling about.

'I'm hoping to find investments that will ensure a secure income for her,' I went on. 'Once I've done that I think I'll be in a position to come back to you and start making practical arrangements.

A tall blonde appeared at the door behind Heraud. She was carrying a Butler's tray upon which stood a china tea pot and all the matching essentials. At first glance I thought it was the receptionist but although she wore a similar blue uniform this girl's name was Helene. Her badge described her as 'Personal Assistant to the General Manager'. She put the tray down on Heraud's desk and then disappeared without saying a word. Heraud poured two cups of tea.

'Milk or lemon?'

'Lemon please.'

'We may be able to help you with your investment programme if you would like us to,' said Heraud, handing me a cup.

I took the cup and looked interested.

'For example, we can help you to arrange an annuity which will ensure that your mother's financial needs are met for the rest of her life.' Heraud opened a drawer in his desk and took out another folder. He placed it on the desk between us.

'An annuity? How does that work?' I asked, hoping that my innocence sounded genuine.

'It's very simple,' said Heraud. 'And utterly reliable. We recommend a company in London which has been in business for over a century and is used by the British Royal Family.'

I looked suitably impressed.

'The insurance company uses your mother's money to buy bonds and other investments which will ensure that she receives a high return on her money for as long as she lives,' said Heraud. 'Depending on the amount involved we can often arrange annuities for people like your mother where the return is as high as 20 to 25% per annum.'

I whistled softly. 'That's very impressive!'

'The only snag with an annuity of any type is, of course, that if anything should ever happen to your mother then the annuity will stop.'

'Oh, naturally.' I agreed. 'But all I'm interested in is making sure that my mother is well looked after. I'm not interested in anything else.'

Heraud started to rub his hands together, then realised what he was doing and stopped. He bent across his desk towards me. 'You'll find the details of the annuity in here,' he said, handing me the brochure that lay on his desk. I put down my cup and took the brochure. 'The next step,' he said, 'is for you to bring your mother along so that we can meet one another.'

I stood up. 'You've been very helpful, Monsieur Heraud. I'm very grateful. I'll take these away with me if I may?' I held up the brochures. Heraud nodded. 'And I hope to be able to get back to you very soon.'

Heraud beamed at me and offered me his hand across the desk. 'It will be an honour if you choose to allow us to look after your mother,' he announced with a slight bow of his head.

He was so good that I almost believed him.

* * *

I telephoned Michael Sunderland from Charles de Gaulle airport that evening.

'Is Barbara there? Did you see her?' he asked when I'd explained where I'd been and why.

'I didn't see her,' I told him. 'But I think she's there.'

'What do we do now?'

'I don't know.' I tried not to sound as weary and depressed as I felt. The truth was that I didn't know what to do next. I was well out of my depth.

'Can we ask the police for help?'

'I've thought of that. But what could I tell them? They're hardly likely to send a search party into a nursing home just because I ask them to.'

'But we've got to do something!'

'I need to get back into the nursing home,' I told him. 'I need to look around properly – to see if I can find Barbara.'

'So, what's the problem?' Michael sounded as impatient as I would have been if I'd been in his shoes.

'I don't know how I'm going to get into the nursing home again. They're expecting me to take my mother with me next time.'

'Can't you?'

'Can't I what?'

'Take your mother with you?'

'Not easily,' I said. 'The only one I had died five years ago.'

'Lizzie!' said Michael suddenly. 'Lizzie will do it.'

'Who's Lizzie?'

'Are you coming back to London?'

63

'My plane leaves in...,' I looked at my watch, '...thirty minutes.'

'Come to my flat as soon as you get back,' said Michael. 'I'll arrange for Lizzie to be there.'

'Who's Lizzie?' I asked.

But I'd run out of money and the telephone was dead.

CHAPTER SIXTEEN

I went straight to Michael's flat.

'How did it go today?' I asked him.

'Slow,' he answered. He seemed to have aged years in the last few days. 'I got another photograph this morning. And another tape.'

'Does she look O.K?'

He nodded.

'Did you see who brought it?'

'They all come by messenger at 6.30 in the morning. It's a different delivery service every morning. I rang one firm but they said that they were paid in cash and didn't know where the packet had come from.'

I looked carefully at the photograph. The contrast with the original photograph of Barbara that Michael had shown me was sharp. Barbara's eyes were full of fear and loneliness.

Michael slipped the cassette into a player and we both stood still and listened to Barbara's shaky voice reading out some dull, impersonal, and to us irrelevant, item of news.

'There's one thing we can count on,' I told him.

Michael looked at me as though already unconvinced.

'The longer the trial lasts the longer we've got to find Barbara. Lonsdale will ensure that they keep sending you pictures and tapes because he wants to keep you happy. He won't let anyone hurt her while the trial is going on. And the longer it goes on the greater my chance of finding Barbara.'

'The way things are going there isn't going to be much question about the result,' said Michael miserably. 'On the evidence that we've seen so far Lonsdale is guilty. I can't see it taking us more than five minutes to reach a decision.'

'You've got to try and make the other jurors doubtful,' I

said. 'Once you all get in that jury room you've got to delay a verdict as long as you can.' Before I could go on the doorbell rang.

'That'll be Lizzie,' said Michael.

'How much does she know?'

'Nothing. I haven't had time to explain anything to her.'

'Can you trust her?'

'She's my sister.' He went to answer the door.

Some people can take over a room the moment they enter it. Lizzie was one of those people. She came into the apartment in a blur, kissing Michael, throwing a plaid cape over the back of the sofa and tossing a huge plastic carrier bag down onto a chair. She waved a hand to me and shook her head to loosen her hair.

Once she stood still it was her hair which took over. It was red and frizzy and there seemed to be yards of it. It was only shoulder length but it surrounded her head like a red blaze. She was in her mid-twenties, about five foot six or five foot seven inches tall and slim. She wore a tartan scarf, a baggy white sweater and a pair of faded blue jeans. Black, calf length boots with huge heels made me realise that she was probably shorter than she looked. She wore no rings and no jewellery. Once I'd got used to her hair I realised that it was her eyes which were her most startling feature. One was bright blue and the other was green. The effect was hypnotic and it was only when she laughed and turned away that I realised that I'd been staring at her without saying anything. It was only when Michael started to tell her what had happened to Barbara that I remembered why he'd invited her over. This was the woman I was supposed to pass off as my mother.

While Michael talked I watched and listened. Lizzie said nothing. She just nodded her head occasionally and shook it from time to time. When he had finished she got up and went across to him, kissed his cheek, put her arms around him and hugged him tightly. I turned away.

'Whatever I can do to help...,' I heard Lizzie say. 'Anything.'

After a few moments silence I turned round and looked at them. Brother and sister. I envied their closeness.

'We need you to play a mother,' said Michael. He nodded towards me. 'His mother.'

I started to say something facetious. I'm not sure what it was going to be. I stopped myself in time.

'O.K.,' said Lizzie, as though Michael had asked her to put the kettle on. She turned to me. 'When? And where?'

'I didn't like to mention the obvious,' I said. 'But don't you think someone might notice that my mother is younger than I am?'

Lizzie smiled.

'Lizzie is an actress,' said Michael. 'She was in Chekhov's Three Sisters at The National last year.'

'But I've got a couple of free days at the moment,' said Lizzie. She laughed. 'I'm 'resting''.

It all seemed impossible but I didn't see what choice I had. Mother substitutes don't grow on trees.

I telephoned the nursing home in Paris. To my surprise there was someone there who could take my call. I explained that I wanted to take my mother along to have a look around and to meet Monsieur Heraud. I fixed an appointment for the following morning.

I said I'd go back to my flat and pick up a couple of things, arrange the tickets and book two rooms in a hotel. Lizzie agreed to meet me later that evening at the check in desk at Heathrow airport.

CHAPTER SEVENTEEN

I always believe in travelling light and I had a spare shirt and a few other odds and ends crammed into a small canvas overnight bag. My toothbrush, razor, passport and tickets were all in the pockets of my old leather jacket. By contrast Lizzie looked as though she was preparing for a trip around the world. In addition to her massive plastic bag she was pushing a trolley holding a huge, old-fashioned carpet bag and a large suitcase.

She smiled and waved furiously when she saw me.

'I brought a few clothes with me,' she explained, noticing the way I looked at her collection of luggage. She was wearing a red felt hat and a trench coat that reached her ankles. When the coat swung open I could see that underneath it she was wearing a black leather mini skirt and a skin tight black sweater. She wore fleur-de-lys patterned tights and shiny black high heeled shoes. She didn't look like anyone's mother – let alone mine.

We joined the queue for our flight to Paris. 'I'll tell them that one of the bags is mine,' I said. 'That way we might get away without having to pay any excess baggage.'

Lizzie put a hand on my arm. 'Do you think Barbara is all right?'

'Yes,' I replied. For the time being I was as confident as I sounded. I didn't know why.

Lizzie squeezed my arm and rested her head against my shoulder for a few seconds. 'Good.' she said faintly. 'I like Barbara.' There was a pause. 'And Michael loves her and I love Michael.'

'You know this could be dangerous, don't you?'

'It doesn't matter.' said Lizzie. 'We've got to do something.'

I should have listened to the way she was saying it as much as to what she said. She sounded like a member of a school girl gang on a summer holiday jape. She was driven by good intentions but perhaps too innocent to realise that good intentions aren't always enough.

From the Charles de Gaulle airport in Paris we caught the Air France bus to the top of the Champs d'Elysée. Alone I would have travelled to the hotel on the underground Metro but the thought of dragging so much luggage around made me feel tired so we picked up a Peugeot taxi from the rank at the top of the Avenue Hoche. The driver was Japanese and he spoke French with the strangest accent I've ever heard.

I'd booked two rooms in a small, anonymous hotel close to the Jardin du Luxembourg on the Left Bank and the drive through Paris and across the Seine excited Lizzie who had never been there before. Our driver, perhaps determined to imitate more traditional Parisian taxi drivers, clearly felt that it was his duty to drive as erratically and as dangerously as possible. Hurtling around the Place de la Concorde at close to 80 kph he missed a coach full of tourists by centimetres. Crossing the Seine onto the Quay Anatole he played 'chicken' with the driver of a large Mercedes and banged his fist on his steering wheel with undisguised delight when the Mercedes driver gave way.

Thankful to be alive I tipped him generously and he surprised me by helping to carry Lizzie's luggage into the hotel.

The hotel was one of the few in Paris not to have been modernised. The duty receptionist, porter and telephone operator was a balding Algerian who could have been anywhere between his early thirties and his late fifties. His upper lip was decorated with a neatly defined black moustache on which he clearly lavished much time and attention. He wore a badly pressed, lightweight fawn suit and had the decaying remains of a red rose bud in his jacket buttonhole.

The only light was provided by a small table lamp which stood on his desk and was connected to the hotel's electricity supply via a lengthy stretch of alarmingly frayed flex. The tiny foyer contained two large leather sofas and three dining chairs. Both the sofas and all the dining chairs were occupied by women who seemed dressed for a party. There were nine of them altogether. The youngest looked about sixteen or seventeen years old. The oldest was probably in her late sixties. Four of them wore long wigs and they all wore a lot of make-up. There was a lot of thigh and a lot of white bosom on view. The oldest stared at Lizzie and our luggage then bent her head towards her neighbour and made a remark which made her companion laugh.

I put my passport down on the desk. 'We've got reservations for two single rooms.'

Using a grubby forefinger to guide his eyes the Algerian looked down the list of scribbled and indecipherable names in the hotel book. He shook his head and told me that I'd made a mistake. I had, he said, only booked one double room. It seemed to amuse him.

I tried arguing with him but he pretended not to understand. He shrugged his shoulders and turned away. The women sitting in the foyer watched with amused interest.

'What's the matter?' asked Lizzie?

'I booked two single rooms,' I explained. 'He says They've only got a double.'

Lizzie didn't seem too worried. 'As long as it's got two beds and a bathroom,' she said.

I asked the Algerian if the room had a bathroom.

He shook his head but assured me that there was one just along the corridor which we could hire by the hour for thirty francs a time.

'There isn't a bathroom,' I told Lizzie, who spoke no French. She smiled weakly and shrugged.

'How many beds does the room have?' I asked the Algerian.

He looked at me as though I'd gone mad. 'One!' he said in heavily accented English. He held up one finger and then pointed it at each of us in turn. He turned towards the two women who were sitting on the nearest sofa and muttered something which made them laugh. I was beginning to feel like a freak show in a circus.

'Does he mean that there's a bed each? asked Lizzie.

'I don't think so.' I felt deeply embarrassed. 'Do you want to try to find somewhere else?'

Lizzie looked at her watch and then at our luggage which took up the remaining space in the foyer. She shook her head.

Just then two North Africans came into the hotel. Both were

wearing blue suits and had their collars unbuttoned. Both had their shirt collars turned neatly over their jacket collars.

At the arrival of the two men the women in the foyer sat up. They smiled, patted their hair and pushed out their chests. One, sitting on one of the dining chairs, crossed and re-crossed her legs slowly and deliberately, unconcernedly revealing her taste in underwear as she did so.

The two men whispered to one another and stared at the women as shoppers might inspect the meat on display in a butcher's shop, pointing out the virtues and drawbacks of each in turn with no regard at all for the usual social niceties.

Lizzie nudged me. 'What's going on?'

The two men, having made their selections, started talking prices.

Lizzie gripped my wrist. 'Am I seeing what I think I'm seeing?'

I turned to the Algerian behind the desk, who seemed totally uninterested in what was going on, and asked him for our key. As I spoke the two men agreed prices and moved towards a bamboo curtain at the rear of the foyer, with their newly chosen companions in tow. The Algerian handed keys to each of the two men as they passed him and then handed a third key to me. Each key was attached by a piece of green string to a large piece of wood.

'Room 17,' he mumbled, as I accepted the key. Then he turned and winked at the abandoned women, who laughed again.

Clutching Lizzie's large suitcase in one hand and carrying my own overnight bag in the other I led Lizzie through the bamboo curtain and up a narrow, dimly-lit staircase. A narrow strip of threadbare, dirty carpet marked the middle of the stairs. Behind us we could hear the women who'd been left behind chattering as they waited for more customers.

'I'm sorry about all this,' I apologised to Lizzie, as I opened the door to our room. It contained a large, old-fashioned bed, a massive wardrobe, a small dressing table and a remarkably small hand-basin which was supplied only by a cold tap. Once we'd put down the luggage there was hardly any room left to move.

Lizzie turned, looked at me and started to giggle. She walked over to the bed and sat down on it. The springs had virtually no resilience left at all and the bed dipped under her alarmingly. Lizzie kicked off her shoes and lay back. The bed creaked noisily and threatened to swallow her up. Lizzie put her hands over her face to try and smother her laughter. The more she laughed the more the bed shook and the more the bed shook the more she laughed.

When we heard the rhythmic creaking of a bed in the room next door I too started to laugh. And when the bed in the room on the other side of us started to creak our laughter came dangerously close to hysterical.

CHAPTER EIGHTEEN

I offered to sleep on the floor but Lizzie wouldn't hear of it. We washed timidly and sparingly in running cold water in our tiny basin (there was no plug with which to block the waste pipe) and then turned off the light and clambered into bed.

It was an uncomfortable night. The mattress was so soft that it constantly tried to throw us both together and to avoid any further embarrassment I spent the night clinging to my side of the bed. At six o'clock in the morning I gave up the unequal struggle, clambered out of bed and wandered downstairs, past the balding Algerian who was sleeping (still in his suit) on one of the sofas in the reception area.

From the hotel I jogged to the Luxembourg Gardens where I ran for thirty minutes among the flower beds and ornamental ponds and fountains. The gravel paths crunched satisfactorily underfoot and the early morning air felt good in my lungs. Then, as half a dozen other early morning joggers invaded the park, I found a quiet grassy spot where I spent another thirty minutes doing press ups and sit ups. I felt much better when I'd finished.

Two streets away I bought a newspaper from a kiosk and found a small café where I ordered a large, steaming bowl of strong coffee and a basketful of fresh croissants. Two of the working girls who'd been waiting in the hotel foyer the evening before were already there having breakfast. They both looked tired and dishevelled, and smiled and laughed a lot as though they'd had a successful night.

At half past eight I went back to the hotel. The Algerian was still sleeping on one of the sofas and across the foyer an elderly woman was sitting on the other sofa. I tiptoed past them and climbed back up the dark and narrow staircase to the room where I'd left Lizzie sleeping. Gently, I pushed the door open.

Lizzie's clothes were strewn around the room and the bed clothes were pulled back but there was no sign of Lizzie at all. I sat down on the edge of the bed and waited. I thought that she'd probably gone along to the bathroom. After five minutes or so I decided to have a shave. After that unpleasant cold water experience I began to get really worried. I walked along the corridor to the bathroom. The door had been left open and the bath had been used but there was no sign of Lizzie. I ran back down the stairs to the foyer. The old woman was the only person there; the balding Algerian had disappeared.

I walked to the front door and looked out into the street. Three girls I hadn't seen before were standing by the wall outside the hotel hoping to pick up some early morning trade. There was no sign of Lizzie. I turned round, went back into the hotel and made my way back towards the staircase.

'Are you looking for a girl?' someone asked me, in broken, halting English.

I half turned. It was the old lady who had spoken. She had grey hair, tied in a bun, and wore a dark dress with a light blue shawl draped around her shoulders.

'A particular girl,' I said. 'An English girl.'

'What does she look like?'

I held a hand at chin level. 'About this tall, very pretty, long red, curly hair.' I realised I didn't have the faintest idea what clothes Lizzie might have been wearing.

'How old?'

'Mid twenties.'

'Are you sure you wouldn't like a younger girl?'

I shook my head. 'No thanks. I need to find this one. Have you seen her?'

The old woman nodded. She adjusted the shawl around her shoulders. She wore woollen gloves with the tips of the fingers cut off. Her movements were slow and deliberate, as though she had arthritis in her joints.

'Where did she go?' I demanded, bending down so that my face was at her level. 'It's important. Did she leave with someone else?'

The old woman just stared at me. She had a cataract developing in her left eye.

I took out my wallet and pulled out a 100 franc note. I folded it and offered it to the old woman. She shook her head. I took out another note and offered the old woman the two. She reached out and took the notes from me. They disappeared somewhere underneath her shawl.

'Well?' I said, impatiently. 'Where did she go?'

'She didn't go anywhere,' said the old woman.

I was losing what remained of my patience. But I still didn't understand.

'Do you always sleep right on the edge of the bed?' demanded the old woman.

'How...?' I started to ask. Then I realised. 'I don't believe it!' I whispered.

'You're not supposed to,' said Lizzie, reverting to her ordinary voice.

'It's brilliant! Absolutely brilliant!' I stared at her. 'But how did you do it? The eyes?'

'I am an actress!' Lizzie reminded me. 'I brought my make-up with me. And a pair of contact lenses.' She smiled. 'Is there anywhere that I can get some breakfast? I'm starving.'

CHAPTER NINETEEN

Heraud was nauseatingly attentive to Lizzie, gently cupping her elbow in his hand as they walked and explaining everything to her in Maurice Chevalier English (his English had been almost accent free when he'd spoken to me alone). I walked behind them, constantly looking for Barbara Sunderland, but seeing no sign of her.

'What do you think?' he asked, when we were all seated in his office. 'Do you think you could be happy with us?' He addressed all his remarks to Lizzie. I thought he had all the convincing charm of a salesman of previously owned motor cars but Lizzie gave the impression that she found him irresistible.

'It's wonderful,' she whispered. 'I'm sure I'll be very happy here.' She lowered her eyes for a moment. 'Are you on duty here all the time, Monsieur Heraud?' she asked coyly. Even I half believed that she was taken with him.

'Certainly I am!' replied Heraud. 'And it will be my pleasure to look after you personally.'

Lizzie examined her gloves and managed to look both embarrassed and delighted. For a moment I thought she was actually going to blush.

'When would you like to move in?' asked Heraud. 'We do have a suite available at the moment but....' He shrugged his shoulders and held his hands palm upwards, indicating that he couldn't promise that the room would be available for long.

Lizzie looked across at me. She seemed flustered and I suspected that some of the fluster was probably genuine. Before I could say anything she looked back at Heraud.

'My son can go back home and collect a suitcase for me,' she

76

said, nodding in my direction. 'If you have a room available I could move into it now.'

I was horrified. This wasn't what we'd planned at all. It was all very well maintaining the deception for half an hour but how on earth was she going to keep it up if she was living in the damned place? What if a maid came in to her room at night? What if a nurse insisted on going into the bathroom with her? And what if a doctor wanted to examine her?

Heraud looked as though he would start purring at any moment.

'Then that's settled,' said Lizzie, sitting back in her chair. She turned to me. 'Will you bring in some of my things?'

'Of course!' I agreed. I didn't seem to have much option.

'There are just a few simple formalities to go through,' said Heraud. He opened a drawer in his desk and took out two large forms. 'First, there is our own contract.' He pushed one of the forms across the desk towards us. 'And second, the form for the annuity which I talked to your son about.' He put the second form on top of the first.

Lizzie picked up the two forms and handed them to me.

The contract with the nursing home was fairly simple. It merely confirmed that the signatory would stay in the nursing home for a minimum of six months and would, after that, give thirty days notice of any intention to leave. The annuity contract was also quite simple. As Heraud had explained to me it offered the signatory a life time income in return for an agreement that upon her death her estate would pass to the company offering the income. The size of the income was, of course, dependent upon the size of the guaranteed assets.

'I'm afraid we can't complete the annuity at the moment,' I said to Heraud. 'I will need to have a meeting with my mother's accountants and solicitors first.'

Heraud threw up his hands. 'Absolutely!' he cried, in mock horror. 'Absolutely! I did not expect your mother to sign this form today.'

'But I'm sure there aren't any problems with the contract,' Lizzie said. She held out a hand for the contract and then for a pen.

Heraud adjusted his tie and held his head slightly to one side, like a cat waiting for a treat. Lizzie scrawled an indecipherable

77

and worthless signature across the bottom of the nursing home contract and I pushed it back across the desk. Heraud had style. He didn't even look at the contract but slid it straight into a drawer with all the sleight of hand of a stage magician. He then stood up, walked around his desk and held out a hand to Lizzie. When she took it he brought his other hand across and buried her fingers in a two handed clasp. 'It's going to be a delight having the honour to look after you,' he said, with a slight bow. 'Now, let me show you to your room.'

I followed them as they left Heraud's office and walked down a long corridor to my 'mother's' new suite.

It was, I had to admit, quite spectacular and a considerable improvement on the grubby hotel room where Lizzie and I had slept the previous night. The sitting room ceiling was high and the plasterwork was magnificent. A crystal chandelier hung from a heavily sculpted fixture in the centre of the ceiling and a marble fireplace dominated one distant wall. The furniture was excellent Louis XV reproduction and three or four good oil paintings in extravagant gilt frames were hung around the walls.

The bedroom and bathroom were equally impressive.

'Everything is carefully designed to our own specification,' Heraud explained proudly. He pointed to the bed. 'The four poster bed looks attractive and decorative,' he said. He waited for Lizzie to nod her agreement. 'But it is built around a standard hospital frame. It has an orthopaedic mattress and is fully adjustable.'

'It's lovely!' beamed Lizzie.

'It is our most expensive suite,' admitted Heraud. 'But it is free at the moment,' he shrugged and smiled. 'And it is perfect for you.'

Lizzie simpered.

'If there is anything you want all you have to do is press one of these buttons.' He pointed to a small red button built onto one side of the bedside cabinet. 'You will find that there are buttons distributed throughout the suite – including a dozen or so at ground level in case of accidents.' He pointed to another red button situated about three inches above floor level by the entrance to the bathroom.

'That's very comforting,' I said.

'I'll leave you now,' said Heraud, rubbing his hands together. He looked at Lizzie. 'I expect you'll want to give your son a list of things that you'd like him to fetch for you.' He backed away towards the door.

When he'd gone I stared at Lizzie for a moment or two. I was furious. 'What the hell are you playing at?' I demanded. 'How are you going to keep this up?' I was angry with her and made no attempt to disguise it. 'This nursing home is owned by Lonsdale,' I reminded her. 'And you know how dangerous he is!' I was angry because I was genuinely concerned.

'Don't be silly,' protested Lizzie. 'Nothing is going to happen. And with me staying here we stand a much better chance of finding Barbara – if she's here.'

'But you won't be just playing a part,' I protested crossly. 'You can't wipe your make-up off after the show and go home. You're going to have to be in character for 24 hours a day.'

'There's nothing to stop me locking the door occasionally,' said Lizzie.

'There are no locks on the doors to this suite,' I pointed out wryly. 'I've already checked.'

Lizzie checked the bathroom door, the bedroom door and then the main entrance door into the suite. She lost some of her colour and her ebullience when she saw that I was right.

'You can stay here today,' I told her. 'And maybe tonight. But then you're coming out again.'

'Not until we've found Barbara!'

'Whether we've found Barbara or not!' I insisted. 'Don't forget Heraud is going to be expecting a signed annuity. How do you think we're going to manage that? Not to mention the fact that we've already signed a contract promising to pay them heaven knows how many thousand francs a night for the next six months.'

'That doesn't matter,' said Lizzie. 'They're crooks anyway.'

'They may not want to take us to court,' I agreed. 'But there are other ways of enforcing payment. And getting you out of here isn't going to be easy now.'

'O.K!' sighed Lizzie, after a long silence. 'If we haven't found Barbara by mid day tomorrow I'll leave.'

'If we can get you out!' I said.

'Stop being so cheerful.' ordered Lizzie. 'Go and get my suitcase – like a dutiful son.'

'What do you want?'

'You'd better bring me my make-up kit and some more old lady clothes.' Lizzie paused. 'And bring me something to wear tonight. You'll have to buy something. I don't think my nightie is quite suitable.'

She was right about that at least.

TWENTY

to the hotel, select the clothes I
lect her make-up and pack her
the hotel while I went to a
ble nightdress.
other,' I told the assistant who
I entered the ladies lingerie

lying and immediately offered
black and diaphanous. I de-
in flannelette.
wrapped and under my arm I
ew more even more personal
f it Lizzie's underwear was
long-sleeved cotton vest, a full
g johns, the most hideous bra
tic stockings. I didn't worry
bought the 'medium' size in

got back to the nursing home

I told the receptionist. 'She

man in her early forties whom
me over fairly carefully and
e I had with me. 'What's in

r my mother.'
eceptionist.
l take it to her myself.'
eptionist.

'I'd like to pop along and make sure she's settled in all right,' I persisted. 'So I might as well take it along.' I didn't want anyone examining the contents of the case. The clothes were no problem but I didn't want anyone finding Lizzie's box of theatrical make-up.

With a scowl the receptionist scribbled my name on a small cardboard badge and handed it to me. 'Would you please wear this.' She turned a visitors' book round and pushed that towards me. 'And would you sign in please.'

I signed the visitors' book, pinned the cardboard badge onto my jacket lapel, assured the receptionist that I could remember which room my mother was staying in and headed off down the corridor. Now that Lizzie had become a resident and we were no longer potential customers who needed to be wooed, the veneer of charm seemed to be a lot thinner.

'What have you got on under that?' I asked Lizzie, handing her the suitcase, and nodding towards the dress she was wearing.

She looked at me as if I'd gone mad so I repeated the question.

'Bra and knickers.'

'Take them off.'

Lizzie giggled. 'Don't tell me you've suddenly decided that you're turned on by shawls and fingerless gloves?'

'There's more suitable underwear in the suitcase,' I told her. 'Go into the bathroom and change. Then give me whatever you've got on and I'll take them out with me. And take the make-up you need and give me what's left.'

'Why? What's the matter?'

'I don't want anyone coming into your room while you're out and discovering your indecent underwear lying around.'

'I don't wear anything indecent!'

'You know what I mean!'

Less than five minutes later I had put Lizzie's own underwear and most of her make-up kit into the suitcase.

'I'm staying here with you,' I told her, fastening the case. 'I'm not leaving you by yourself.'

'Don't be silly! You'll blow everything!'

'Don't worry – I'll convince the receptionist that I've left.'

When I got back to the foyer the receptionist was talking to someone on the telephone. She seemed surprised to see me so quickly. She put her hand over the mouthpiece. 'That was a short visit!'

'I'm just taking this suitcase out to the car,' I explained. 'It's some bits and pieces that she's decided she doesn't need.'

'You don't have to do that,' said the receptionist. 'We've got plenty of storage space.'

'It's my case,' I lied. 'I might need it.'

'Can I have your badge?' asked the receptionist.

'I'm coming back in a moment.'

'I'm not allowed to let you out of the nursing home with a badge on,' said the receptionist. She looked at her watch. 'I'm going off duty in a few minutes and I have to keep the visitors book up to date.'

I took the badge off and handed it to her. Then I walked briskly outside to the car park. I wanted to get back into the hospital again as quickly as I could.

I'd arrived in a taxi but I didn't take long to find a brand new Citroën with the boot open. I dumped the suitcase into the boot and walked quickly back into the nursing home. I grinned inanely at the receptionist. 'Hello again! Can I have my badge back?'

The receptionist held my badge out to me and got me to sign the book again.

When I got back to Lizzie's suite she seemed to have disappeared. I called her name and she appeared out of the bedroom dressed in the new underwear I'd bought her. She had been laughing a lot and her eye make-up had run, leaving long black streaks down her cheeks. The elastic stockings were too big for her and had collapsed into wrinkles around her ankles.

I waited two minutes, picked up a plastic bag that had contained some of Lizzie's new clothes, filled it with towels and then walked briskly back down the corridor towards the reception desk.

The receptionist sighed when she saw me. I handed her my visitors badge, signed the book again and hurried outside. I walked round the car park, threw the bag into the boot of the same Citroën and then went back inside. The receptionist was busy talking to a new girl who was, I assumed, the relief receptionist.

'Shan't be long!' I said breathlessly. 'Just another minute or two.' I was getting confused and I was pretty sure the receptionist was too.

'O.K.' said the receptionist wearily. She waved me through impatiently and carried on talking to the new girl who ignored me totally. I walked briskly past her, headed down the corridor and let myself into Lizzie's room with no visitor's badge and without having signed the visitors' book.

'Which do you think?' Lizzie asked me, holding up two dark coloured dresses that I found virtually indistinguishable.

I pointed to the one on the left.

'I need somewhere to hide if anyone comes in,' I said, looking around the room.

'Why this one?' asked Lizzie, frowning. 'What's wrong with the other one?'

'It isn't your colour.' I opened a large cupboard to the left of the fireplace. If I took the shelf out there would be just enough room for me to get into the cupboard in an emergency.

'I think you ought to stay in the bedroom,' said Lizzie. 'Then if someone comes in you'll have more time to hide. There's a massive, walk-in wardrobe in there.' She stepped into the dress I'd turned down. 'If you're in here and someone walks in you won't have time to get into the cupboard.' She turned round. 'Fasten me up will you?' The back of the dress had a row of hooks and eyes.

'No!' I said firmly. 'If you can't fasten it yourself then an old woman certainly wouldn't be able to.'

'You're right,' agreed Lizzie, slipping out of the dress. She picked up its competitor, which had a much easier fastening. 'I preferred this one all along.'

'I'll go into the bedroom.' I said, with a sigh.

CHAPTER TWENTY-ONE

I woke up with a start. It was semi-dark and I couldn't remember where I was.

An old lady with a cataract in one eye was shaking my shoulders. She wore a shapeless, pink, flannelette nightgown.

'Come on!' she whispered. 'It's three o'clock.'

Slowly I remembered.

'Hello, Lizzie.' I yawned.

'I thought the idea of coming in here was to look for Barbara?'

I sat up with a start, stretched, threw back the sheets and clambered out of bed. 'Where did you sleep?'

'There!' said Lizzie, pointing to the other side of the bed I'd just left. 'That's twice we've spent the night together and you haven't even made a pass at me.' She grinned. 'Maybe one of us ought to be worried.'

Five minutes later I was dressed and as alert as I was ever going to be. I opened the door from the living room to the corridor a fraction of an inch and listened carefully.

'Let me,' hissed Lizzie, pushing me aside. She was still wearing her nightdress.

I tried to hold her back. 'You stay here!'

'It'll be damned sight easier for me to explain what I'm doing than it will be for you.'

She was right. She poked her head out through the doorway and looked up and down the corridor. 'There's no one about,' she said. She hesitated for a moment and then turned left. 'Let's try this way first.'

After about twenty yards the corridor reached a junction. We had a choice of right or left.

'We went down there this morning,' I said, nodding to the left. 'Let's try this way.' I turned right. Lizzie followed.

Most of the doors in the nursing home were clearly marked. High up on each door was a metal plaque stating the room's name. (Lizzie's room was the Versailles Suite). Underneath the metal plaque there was a metal card holder in which the name of the occupant was written.

'Yesterday morning,' said Lizzie.

I turned. 'What?'

'It was yesterday morning that we went on our tour,' whispered Lizzie. 'You said this morning.'

I sighed. Pedantry was a luxury I didn't really feel we had time for.

All the doors in this corridor bore a metal plaque. But instead of names the white cards simply carried numbers. I turned the door handle to the first door. It was unlocked. But then I noticed that each door had a tiny spy hole fitted just underneath the metal card holder. The cover across the spy hole was on the outside so that whoever was inside couldn't see out. I moved the cover, put my eye against the spy hole and looked in. Nothing. The light was on but the room was empty.

The next two spy holes I looked through were similarly unproductive. But at the fourth attempt I hit the jackpot. A young woman whom I instantly recognised as Barbara Sunderland was lying asleep just a few yards from the door. A small overhead lamp illuminated the room which was much smaller and much more simply furnished than Lizzie's room.

I signalled for Lizzie to look through the spy hole. Excitedly she turned to me. 'That's her!'

I tried the door handle. To my surprise, it moved easily and the door opened soundlessly. I moved swiftly into the room and signalled to Lizzie to shut the door behind us.

A few seconds later, with the door closed, we both heard the sound of a lock being operated. Turning away from the bed, where Barbara was still asleep, I tried the door handle. The door wouldn't budge. We'd found Barbara all right. But now we were prisoners with her.

CHAPTER TWENTY-TWO

The room in which Barbara was being kept prisoner was much simpler and less expensively furnished than the suite Heraud had provided for Lizzie but it was equipped with every necessity for good medical and nursing care.

Mounted on a shelf beside Barbara's bed was a small monitor connected to the nursing home's computerised records system that Heraud was so proud of. Underneath the computer monitor was an intravenous feed source designed so that instead of having to connect patients up to bottles of fluid hanging upside down from drip stands nurses and doctors could simply connect their patients directly to a central supply. Finally there was a gas supply point – presumably provided so that doctors or nurses could supply oxygen or anaesthetic gases.

Lizzie went straight across to the bed and put her arm around Barbara who had begun to wake up when we'd entered the room. Barbara looked terrified but didn't utter a sound. She had the knuckles of her right hand pressed into her mouth.

'It's me – Lizzie!'

Barbara didn't look convinced.

'If you want her to believe you,' I whispered urgently. 'You'd better take some of that make-up off.'

Lizzie tore her wig off and shook her head so that her own hair came free. The she bent her head, cupped her hand underneath her right eye and allowed the first contact lens to fall out. Then she did the same thing with the other contact lens.

'Lizzie? Is that really you?' Barbara whispered. 'What are you doing here?' She took her hand away from her mouth and reached up to touch Lizzie's shoulder, as though checking that she was real. Then she remembered me. 'Who's he?' she asked. She looked confused as well as frightened.

'He's a friend of Michael's,' said Lizzie. 'We've come to help get you out of here.'

Barbara burst into tears. She threw her arms around Lizzie's neck and her body shook as she began to sob uncontrollably.

'How long have you been here?' I asked Barbara.

She shook her head and whispered that she didn't know.

'Did they bring you here after they took you from the café?'

'They told me that Michael had collapsed and was being taken to hospital,' said Barbara. 'They said they'd taken him out through the back of the café to avoid upsetting all the other customers.' She spoke so quietly that I could hardly hear her. I had to move forwards until I was almost touching her.

Lizzie got up from the bed, where she'd been sitting along-side Barbara, and went over to the door. She tried the handle. It moved but the door didn't open.

'He hadn't had he? said Barbara. 'Is he all right?'

For a moment I didn't know what she meant.

'No!' I said, at last. 'Michael hadn't collapsed. He's fine.' As quickly and as concisely as I could I explained to her why she'd been kidnapped.

'Will they hurt him?' Barbara wanted to know.

I shook my head. 'Certainly not while the trial goes on. Nor will they hurt you.' Then I turned my attention to our more immediate problem. 'When we came in the door locked after us,' I told Barbara. I couldn't think of a more encouraging way to put it.

'You mean we're all locked in here now?'

I nodded.

Silent tears started to roll down Barbara's cheeks as her newfound hopes began to disappear.

'He'll think of something,' said Lizzie, nodding in my direction and speaking with surprising confidence. She moved towards the bathroom. 'Since I no longer have to pretend to be your mother I'm going to clean off some of this gunk.'

I looked at my watch. It was ten to four. 'What time do they bring you breakfast?' I asked Barbara.

'Half past seven, I think.'

'Trust you to think of your stomach,' said Lizzie, coming out of the bathroom, using a towel to wipe her face clean.

I walked across the room, checked the door again and then examined the window. Like Lizzie's suite the room was on the ground floor but the window here had a heavy iron grid across it on the outside. Unless Barbara had an assortment of power tools tucked under her bed we wouldn't be getting out that way. I didn't think the power tools were much of a possibility so I ignored that option and went into the bathroom. This time the window was smaller and made of frosted glass. But it was also covered with a heavy iron grid.

I went back to the bedroom and sat down on the only chair.

'Is the door still locked?' asked Lizzie.

I nodded.

'Can we get out through the window?'

'No. It's barred.'

'What about the bathroom?'

'The same.'

'You could stand behind the door and hit whoever brings the breakfast tray in over the head with the chair,' suggested Lizzie brightly.

About ten minutes later both Lizzie and Barbara began to giggle. I looked at them in surprise but before I could say anything to them I found myself giggling too. Just before I passed out I realised that someone outside the room had turned on the gas supply and was using it to anaesthetise us all. I remember trying to reach the gas supply point to block it but before I could do anything I collapsed onto the floor.

Laughing gas.

But it wasn't funny.

CHAPTER TWENTY-THREE

I felt sick and my head ached. I shivered, opened my eyes and looked around. It was dark and I was lying on something hard. I could hear voices. I tried to roll over onto my side and caught sight of the sky. The silhouette of a distant building and a few close, shadowy figures backlit by a street lamp dominated my field of view. I was, I realised, lying outside on a road. I must have had an accident.

Suddenly I felt my ankles being gripped. I reached to find something to hold onto but my fingers scratched uselessly and painfully at the surface of the road. The person holding my ankles pulled me along the road. I felt my clothes tearing. My head banged on the road and I temporarily lost consciousness.

'Now the ribs!' I heard someone say a little later. A heavily booted foot landed on my chest. I bent double with the pain, retching uselessly.

'Now the feet!' said the same voice. 'I need a shoe and a sock off and a cut or a heavy graze.'

I felt someone's hands sliding under my armpits and then I was being pulled along the road again.

'Loosen his shoe laces,' a second voice suggested. 'His shoes are too bloody tight.'

Whoever it was who was pulling me lowered my body to the road, unfastened and then retied my shoe laces. This time, as I was dragged along the road, I felt my shoes slip off. Then I felt a sock sliding down my foot.

'Great!' said the voice again. 'Now a nice cut. I need a vein.'

I opened my eyes and tried desperately to focus on what was happening. I felt dizzy and nauseated, as though I was coming round after an operation. I shivered again and felt a few spots of rain on my face.

'How about this?' I heard someone say.

'What is it?'

'Bit of broken beer bottle by the looks of it.'

'Fine. Give it to me.'

I felt something stab at my foot. I tried to sit up but I felt too weak.

'He's coming round again shall I give him another whiff of gas?'

'No. Leave him now. I won't be long.'

With a great effort I managed to sit up. I balanced myself precariously on my elbows. I could see three men. One of them was crouched over a small black case. He removed a glass phial from the case, checked it and then neatly snapped off the end. I could feel something warm and sticky running over my foot.

'He's awake, doc!' I heard someone say.

The crouching figure looked across at me and grinned.

'I don't think we've met,' he said. My name is Simpson. Dr Simpson.' He carefully stood the phial up on the road and then reached into the black case again. 'We've been following you ever since you came out of The Grand with Michael Sunderland,' he said. He took out a plastic syringe to which he attached a needle. I watched him.

'You'll like this,' continued Simpson. 'I'm rather proud of it.' He laughed, dipped the needle into the phial and started to draw the fluid up into the syringe.

I just stared.

'This is potassium chloride solution,' explained the doctor. 'Given normally it stimulates the heart,' he held the syringe up against the street light and squinted at it, checking to see that it didn't contain any air bubbles. He pressed the plunger on the syringe. A thin stream of liquid shot from the needle. 'But,' he continued, 'if injected rapidly it causes an almost instantaneous heart attack.'

I felt cramp developing in my left arm. I shifted position slightly.

'The beauty of it is that it is impossible to trace afterwards,' said Simpson. 'If they do a post mortem on you all they'll find is that you've had a heart attack.

'Needle marks,' I croaked. My throat felt dry and rough. 'Haven't you forgotten about the needle marks?'

'Not at all,' said Simpson, looking and sounding very pleased with himself. 'When you were hit by that car you were dragged along the road and you cut your foot on a piece of broken glass – the glass went straight through a vein.'

I moved a little and looked at my feet. They seemed a thousand miles away. Slowly they came into focus. It was strange. My feet had always been loyal to me before. I could see that my left foot was naked and there was a large cut near the ankle bone. Blood was oozing out and making quite a mess.

'I'm going to inject the potassium chloride straight into the open vein,' said Simpson. 'No needle marks and no trace of the drug. You'll be dead within five minutes.'

I swallowed hard. Slowly, triggered by anxiety and the proximity of death my mind started to work faster and faster. I remembered being in Barbara's room at the nursing home. I remembered Lizzie. And Michael. The court case. Lonsdale and Simpson. I remembered Lindsay too. Strangely, I remembered being a boy scout in the local troop.

A thousand images competed for attention. Lizzie, dressed in the flannelette nightie. Barbara, frightened and tearful. Lindsay, confident and elegant. Me, dressed in shorts and long socks with badges proudly worn on my shirt. Michael climbing out of his BMW. The half empty flat in St John's Wood.

'There isn't much time, doctor,' said one of the others.

I looked around. Was it my imagination or was it getting lighter? Snakes. I remembered the country survival classes I'd attended as a boy. 'The markings on the back of an adder snake make it easy to distinguish from a grass snake'. I remembered the scout master, an elderly school teacher who left in disgrace a few years later after some offence that no one would talk about. I could hear his voice. Pompous and dry. 'The adder, Vipera Berus, is our only poisonous snake. It is found throughout mainland Great Britain in dry and open country and easily identified by the dark zigzag stripe down its back.' I tried to concentrate on what was happening.

'Get into the car,' Simpson said to people I couldn't see. 'Get the engine started. He nodded towards the black case. 'And take that.'

The other men did as they were told. I heard a car engine start and then heard it ticking over. It sounded like a diesel engine.

'The grass snake is easily recognised by the pale ring round its neck.' I could hear the scout master again. 'The longest grass snake ever found in Britain was 1.75 metres long. The legless lizard is often mistaken for a snake but it is quite harmless. The only poisonous snake in Britain is the adder. It hibernates from mid October to late February. The young are born from eggs that hatch sometime in August or September. Nesting adders don't like to be disturbed. Tread carefully when walking in dry, open country. If you tread on one the bite can kill you. Adders rarely bite except when disturbed.'

Simpson was bending down and concentrating on the syringe. I felt the needle working its way into my foot. Strangely, it didn't hurt. I tried to push Simpson away but he just stopped what he was doing for a moment and pushed me back with his left hand. I felt desperately weak as well as sick and faint. I felt bile rising in my throat. There wasn't time to be sick. I tried to think; tried to get my mind into motion again. The scoutmaster came back. 'As long as you put a tourniquet on quickly – and don't leave it there for too long – you can stop the poison reaching your heart.'

'Stop the poison reaching your heart.'

My brain was working so fast that everything else seemed to be operating in slow motion. I watched Simpson stand up, the syringe still in his hand, and then watched him hurry away in the direction of the diesel engined motor car. I needed a tourniquet.

'What can you use as a tourniquet?' It was the scout master again.

'A belt, sir!' I heard my own bright, youthful voice.

'Excellent! A belt.'

I unbuckled my trouser belt and tore it free. Trembling with the effort I sat up and wound the belt around my thigh. Once. Twice. Then I fastened it as tight as I could get it. Tighter. So tight that it hurt. It had to hurt.

I collapsed back on the road. My leg already felt numb.

'Now what?'

My brain was still racing. 'Cut above the wound to drain the poison.'

Cut. A knife. I needed a knife. I reached into my jacket pocket for my penknife. Gone. A piece of glass would do.

They'd talked about a broken bottle. The growl of the diesel engine grew fainter as Simpson's car disappeared. I looked around and found the piece of broken glass that Simpson had used to cut my foot. How long had I got? Where did I need to cut? Venous blood travels up the leg.

If I stood up the potassium chloride would take longer to reach my heart. I needed to stand up. I struggled to my knees and then to my feet. I wobbled but managed to stay upright.

I needed a cut at the top of my leg. I couldn't pull my trousers down because of the belt fastened around my thigh. I slashed at the fabric of my trousers with the broken piece of glass. The glass pierced the cloth and scratched my leg. I slashed again until a large area of skin was visible. I needed the biggest vein I could find. If only I had varicose veins. What's the longest vein called? I tried to think back to school. Biology with Miss Crawshaw. The longest vein in the human body is the saphenous vein. It runs up the inside of the thigh alongside the artery. What's that called. The femoral artery.

I felt dizzy and started to fall. I staggered off the road and onto the pavement. There was a doorway a few yards away. I almost fell into it. I stabbed the inside of my thigh with the broken bottle. Not hard enough. It had to be done. The potassium chloride was travelling up my leg. I could almost feel it coursing along my veins. I stabbed hard. I mustn't hit an artery. Arteries carry blood away from the heart; down the leg. Dark red blood poured out over the broken glass in my hand. How much blood could I afford to lose? How much does the body contain? Eight or ten pints? So how much is there in a leg? Two pints perhaps? What does two pints of blood look like?

I slid down the shop door and sat in a growing puddle of my own blood on the pavement. I felt very tired and wanted to sleep.

*   *   *

When I woke the blood I had lost had congealed and I found myself sitting in a warm, sticky, darkening mess. Woken by a throbbing pain in my left leg I opened my eyes and looked around. The sun was beginning to show itself above the horizon and I could see that the road I was on was bigger and busier than I had thought. As dawn broke so commuters preparing for a day's work in the city started to trundle along to somewhere. I didn't know where.

I wanted nothing more than to sleep. I wanted to curl up and to forget the world. I didn't want to think about my leg. I didn't want to think about dying.

And then I remembered Simpson. And I remembered Lizzie and Barbara. Instinctively, but hesitantly, I put a hand on the left hand side of my chest. I could feel my heart still beating. I took as deep a breath as I could. I could feel some pain from my ribs but nothing else. Besides, pain meant that I was still alive.

I tried to move but couldn't. My left leg was numb. I wondered how long the tourniquet had been on. I peered down at my leg, wiped away some of the sticky blood with my hand and stared down at the wound I had made. It was rough and deep.

I knew I had to release the tourniquet to let some fresh, clean blood into the tissues. I would have to put some pressure on the wound to cut down the amount of bleeding. Already I felt faint and I knew that I couldn't afford to lose much more blood. I looked in my pockets for a handkerchief but couldn't find one. In the end I just put the palm of my right hand onto the wound in my thigh and then unfastened the belt that had been stopping the blood from getting through.

I felt the blood rush into my leg and couldn't stop myself screaming out with pain as the blood surged again into the tissues. I felt blood seeping out between my fingers and, looking down, saw blood escaping from the cut on my foot. After a few moments my leg began to feel close to normal again. I refastened the tourniquet but left it a little looser this time. With great difficulty I pulled myself up onto my feet. I knew I needed to get help fast. Clinging to the wall I edged out onto the pavement and stared out at the road.

The cars and lorries streamed past without slowing down. I waved feebly at them but they either did not see me or else, more likely, they simply chose to ignore me. Finally, exhausted and unable to stand any longer, I fell forwards onto the road.

CHAPTER TWENTY-FOUR

Heraud stared right at me and squeezed the trigger of the automatic he was holding.

Click.

He squeezed the trigger again.

Click.

Angrily Heraud kept squeezing. Click. Click. Click. Click.

The magazine was empty.

While Heraud reloaded I threw myself to one side in an attempt to escape. I felt someone gently but firmly hold me still. I could smell her perfume and I could hear her voice.

'It's all right!' she said, over and over again. 'It's all right. It's all right.'

I opened my eyes and looked around. Everything seemed white. The first thing I saw was the ceiling. That was white. The walls were white too. The sheets on the bed were white. The nurse was dressed in white. The nurse.

The nurse was holding me still and it was clearly taking all the effort she could raise to restrain me. She looked about eighteen. She had dark brown eyes, a round, almost child-like face, and large, soft looking lips.

'It's all right.' she said again.

'Where am I?'

The nurse looked puzzled. 'Ne comprends pas!' she said. 'Parlez-vous français?'

'I'm sorry. Where am I?' I looked around. A half full plastic bag of blood hung upside down from a hook on a long metal stand that stood by the foot of my bed. The blood was connected to my arm via a length of plastic tubing.

'L'Hotel Dieu,' replied the nurse. 'You were brought here this morning.'

'What time is it?'

I felt confused. I could remember Lizzie and Barbara. I could remember lying on the road. I could remember someone with a syringe.

The nurse looked at a small, cheap metal watch that was pinned upside down on the front of her uniform. She seemed frightened to let me go.

'It's all right,' I said. 'I won't move. You can let me go.'

Slowly, cautiously, the nurse took her arms off my chest. 'It's a quarter to three,' she said.

I looked towards the windows. The sun was shining. Quarter to three in the afternoon.

'When was I brought here?'

'This morning.'

I looked down. Several leads were attached to my chest. They were connected to a large grey metal box that stood on a grey metal cabinet by the side of my bed. There was a small screen on the front of the box and a green line constantly traced what I recognised as the electrical contractions of my heart. Every time my heart beat the metal box emitted a reassuring 'click'.

Click. Click. Click.

'Do you know what happened?'

The nurse shook her head. 'Are you sure you're going to be sensible?' she looked doubtful. 'You won't move?'

I smiled at her.

'I'll get the doctor,' said the nurse. She moved away from the bed, keeping her eyes on me for as long as she could. 'I won't be a minute.'

'O.K.,' I said, still smiling at her.

Slowly, images were returning to my mind. I could remember lying in a doorway. I could remember being bitten by a snake. I could remember jabbing myself with a piece of broken glass. I felt beads of sweat on my forehead as the memory came back. I felt the crisp, clean bed sheets constricting my chest. I could see Heraud now with the syringe in his hand. No snake.

'Hey! You promised!' The nurse was back. Gently, she held me still. She half turned, took a tissue from a box that lay on a small table behind her and wiped the sweat from my forehead.

'Hello!' said a tall man dressed in a white coat. 'I'm going to give you an injection. It'll help you to relax.'

I stared at him in horror. The doctor bending over me was holding a syringe. It was Dr Simpson. Where the hell was I? I must have been taken back to the nursing home. I shouted his name in terror and then screamed.

CHAPTER TWENTY-FIVE

Slowly, I opened my eyes. The fluorescent light tube on the ceiling was humming. The curtains were drawn.

Click. Click. Click.

That was the heart monitor. I knew that. I was in hospital. I was alive.

I looked to my left. The blood filled bag had gone and so had the plastic tubing in my arm. I turned to my right. No one. Where was the nurse?

I moved an arm. It felt fine. I moved my right leg. That felt fine. I moved my other arm. That felt fine too. There was just my left leg to try. I tried to move it and it felt fine. But I'd heard of people who'd had limbs amputated still thinking that their limbs were attached. I had to look at it. I lifted back the sheets. I was dressed in a white hospital nightshirt that ended just above my knees. Two normal looking legs poked out from beneath it. My left foot was heavily bandaged.

I reached down, picked up the hem of the nightshirt and slowly pulled it upwards. Another stretch of bandage appeared. I touched it. The leg was sore but it was still there.

'Hello!' said someone suddenly. 'Just checking to see you haven't lost anything?'

I turned. A woman in her early thirties was standing in the doorway. She wore an unbuttoned white coat and had her hands stuffed in her coat pockets. A stethoscope hung around her neck. She was wearing a plain blue skirt that was a good six inches shorter than her white coat and a white blouse which was buttoned up to the neck. She had short blond hair cut in a pageboy style and had sharp, piercing blue eyes that seemed to be laughing.

'Hello!' I said, hastily pulling my nightshirt down and pulling the sheets back up.

'It's all right!' said the woman doctor. 'You needn't worry. You haven't got anything that I haven't already seen.' She stepped into the room, took her hands out of her pockets and folded her arms across her chest. 'I'm Dr Berland. I was on duty when you were brought in this morning. How are you feeling now?'

'Fine. And thank you.'

'You had some very strange injuries.'

I wondered what to tell her. Would she believe me?

'You seem to have been stabbed in the thigh with a piece of glass,' said the doctor. 'Were you in a fight?'

If I told her the truth she would want to tell the police. I didn't want that.

'I don't remember.' I said. I was lying a lot these days. Now I was even doing it to doctors. 'My mind is a blank.'

'We cleaned up the wound as best we could,' said Dr Berland. 'We gave you a tetanus shot and some penicillin.' She uncrossed her arms and put her hands back into her pockets.

I wanted to sleep again.

'You lost a lot of blood,' said Dr Berland. 'We had to give you three pints. You are a very healthy man. Very fit. Otherwise you would have died.'

'I'm very grateful to you for all that you've done. Thank you.'

'You also had two broken ribs,' said Dr Berland. 'We just strapped them up. There was no internal damage.'

I felt my chest. I could feel the strapping underneath the nightshirt. I moved my shoulders and bent my arms. I felt weak.

'You were found on the road,' said Dr Berland. 'A lorry driver stopped and brought you in. He nearly ran over you. You were very lucky.'

It was, I thought, about time I had a few lucky breaks. 'Do you know what time it is now?' I asked her.

'Half past ten,' said Dr Berland, without looking at her watch.

'When can I leave the hospital?'

'Maybe tomorrow. There isn't anything seriously wrong

100

with you. I stitched the two cuts but I used dissolving stitches. They will disappear by themselves.'

'There isn't anything wrong with my heart?'

Dr Berland shook her head. 'No. Why? Should there be?' She looked puzzled for a moment. 'I'll get the nurse to come and disconnect you from the monitor,' she said. 'It was just a precaution.'

'Did I have any money on me when I was found?'

'A little. And some credit cards. They are in your bedside cabinet with your passport.' Dr Berland nodded towards the cabinet on the far side of the bed.

They would have wanted my body to be identified.

'I'll need some clothes.'

'You'll certainly need some new trousers. We had to throw yours away. They were beyond repair.'

'Would it be possible for you to get some for me?'

'No. I can't go out shopping. I'm on duty. And even if I could I don't think that there would be any clothes shops open at this time of night – even in Paris.'

'It's important that I leave the hospital tonight.' I said.

'You should stay until tomorrow. Just a few hours ago you were so confused that you screamed when one of my colleagues approached. You kept calling him Dr Simpson. Who is Dr Simpson? Is he your normal doctor?'

'No.' I paused. 'As you said I must have been confused.'

Dr Berland unfolded her arms, reached down and picked up my left wrist. Apparently satisfied with my pulse she nodded briskly, dropped my hand and turned away. Just before she reached the door she turned round. 'If you remember what happened to you perhaps you'd be kind enough to let me know,' she said. 'I have an obligation to report incidents to the police if I think they should be involved.'

After Dr Berland had disappeared I waited a quarter of an hour and then carefully folded back the bed sheets and swung my legs round to one side of the bed. I winced as I put my weight on my feet. The whole of my left leg seemed to throb with pain. I stood for a moment, feeling dizzy and rather nauseated, and then gingerly took a few steps towards the window. The pain in my leg was constant but just bearable.

I opened the bedside cabinet and removed my wallet and

passport. Then, wearing only my hospital nightshirt I padded silently round the cold floor of the room until I was confident that I could walk without falling over. I tiptoed to the door and looked up and down the corridor outside.

Twenty five minutes later I walked out of the hospital wearing a cheap suit that was several sizes too small. I had bought it from a patient in a nearby room for an outrageous sum.

CHAPTER TWENTY-SIX

Crouched in the bushes a hundred yards away from the nursing home entrance I peered through the rain. Most of the nursing home was in darkness but two rooms to the right of the entrance were ablaze with light. I closed my eyes and tried to work out which rooms they were. The rain had long since soaked through my ill-fitting suit and I shivered uncontrollably. My leg was throbbing and I felt faint with hunger. I couldn't remember when I had last eaten.

Cautiously, I moved to my left. I wanted to get into the building as far away as possible from the lights. Bent almost double I ran along behind a neatly clipped hedge. The rain, hammering down on the leaves of the horse chestnut trees above drowned the sound of my feet squelching on the wet grass.

The side of the nursing home was now in view. It was completely dark apart from a single light burning in an upstairs room. I came out from behind the hedge and moved forwards carefully, half scaring myself to death as I bumped into a small statue of a faun.

I brushed sodden hair back from my forehead and wiped my eyes with a soaking wet jacket sleeve. I blinked and moved forwards swiftly. Seconds later I was standing with my back to the wall of the nursing home.

There was no point in standing around in the rain any longer. I had to get inside. I turned towards the nearest window. It was an old-fashioned sash window but three metal bars had been set into the stonework outside it. For a moment I was surprised. I hadn't remembered seeing any bars on the room Lizzie had been in. Then I remembered that the room where Barbara had been held prisoner had barred windows. From inside the metal bars had looked new and solid but a close examination showed that they were thinner than they looked. They were, however, far too strong to break or bend.

Tentatively, I reached between the bars and tried to push the bottom half of the sash window up. It didn't move. Without hesitating I took off my jacket and rolled it around my fist. Then I banged my sheathed fist against the glass. At the third attempt it broke. After waiting in silence for a minute or so I removed my hand from inside my coat and picked the remaining sharp pieces of glass from the window frame. I could feel my heart thumping; the noise it was making seemed loud enough to wake the whole of Paris.

'Barbara?' I called quietly.

There was no reply.

'Lizzie?'

Again, silence.

With impatience and frustration building up inside me I banged my fist against the stone wall of the nursing home. I felt tired. I was hungry. My leg was hurting. I didn't really know what I was doing there. I should have been back home looking for another job.

I moved away from the broken but impenetrable window. A dozen yards to the right I found another similar window. This time there were no bars. Again I wrapped my coat around my fist to break the glass and reached inside to unfasten the catch holding the sash in place.

I slid the window up a couple of feet. It creaked and stuck a little to start with but soon began to move more easily. When the gap was wide enough I pulled myself up onto the window sill and slid head first into the room on the other side.

Once inside I stood still for a moment, listening for any sounds that might suggest that my break in had been heard. But I could hear nothing other than my own heavy breathing and my own heart beating.

The door from the room into the corridor was unlocked and I slowly opened it just far enough to see into the corridor.

It was as dark as the room had been and seemed quite deserted. I turned to my right and cautiously tiptoed along to the next door. By now my eyes were more accustomed to the darkness. I opened the door and peered into the room. It contained nothing apart from an empty bed, a chair and a wardrobe.

How many rooms were there, I wondered? How many doors would I have to open to find Lizzie and Barbara?

Now that I was inside it seemed an impossible task. I had no idea where to look. Outside I'd felt sure that the room with the bars on the windows was the room where Barbara had been held. But how many rooms were there with windows with bars on?

Worse still, I was risking discovery every time I opened a door. Sooner or later I was bound to open a door to a room that was occupied by some nervous old lady who would scream the minute I poked my head around her door. Then the element of surprise – my only advantage – would be lost.

I decided to head straight for the front part of the building where I'd seen the bright lights. That was where Heraud's office was. With luck Heraud would be there.

CHAPTER TWENTY-SEVEN

Heraud was alone when I walked in. When he saw me he opened his mouth but said nothing. It would be an understatement to say that he looked surprised.

'Where are Barbara and Lizzie?' I asked him. I'd stopped dripping water but my soaked suit was now steaming.

Heraud said nothing.

'Michael Sunderland's wife and the woman I came here with,' I said. 'Where are they?'

'You should be dead.' said Heraud, still stunned.

'So should you. But neither of us is. So, where are they?'

'Why the hell should I tell you anything?' demanded Heraud. I noticed that despite the air conditioning he was beginning to sweat.

I moved forwards a few feet. 'Because if you don't I'll kill you.' I was surprised to hear myself say it and even more surprised to realise that I might mean it. I felt cold and surprisingly calm inside.

Heraud started to move to his left, trying to get a little closer to the door. I moved to my right and cut him off.

'You can't get away a second time,' said Heraud.

'You didn't think I'd get away the first time,' I reminded him. I took two paces forward and gripped the front of Heraud's immaculate jacket in my right hand. I then lifted him upwards until he was standing on tiptoe. I lowered my head an inch or two so that my eyes were almost on a level with his. 'Where are they?' I asked him quietly.

'They've been moved,' said Heraud, his face going slightly blue. There was terror in his eyes and I realised that Heraud was not a brave man.

'Why would you have moved them? You all thought I was

dead.' I increased the pressure around Heraud's throat. He pulled at my hands with his fingers but he was weak and out of condition.

'You knew where the Sunderland woman was,' Heraud pointed out. 'You might have told someone.' He struggled ineffectively. 'I can't breathe!' he protested.

I ignored him 'Where are they?'

'In another nursing home,' said Heraud still clawing at my hands. 'Don't kill me,' he pleaded. 'Please don't kill me!'

'Which one?'

'I don't know.'

I pulled my left hand back a couple of feet and jabbed him sharply in the stomach. At the same time I let go of his jacket. He collapsed onto his knees, wheezing and gasping for breath.

'Where are they?' I asked him again.

'I don't know,' wheezed Heraud, bent double. 'Dr Simpson decided where to send them.'

I hit him on the side of the head with the flat of my hand. 'When did they leave?'

'Last night,' said Heraud, sobbing. He rubbed at his stomach and then at his head. He looked up at me. I could see the tears on his cheeks. 'A car came for them last night.' Alone and frightened he had none of his normal superficial charm and arrogance.

I reached down, grasped hold of his left shoulder and pulled him to his feet. I put my hand around his throat.

'I don't know where they've gone,' he said, terror in his eyes. I believed him. I didn't think he'd have the courage to lie to me. 'Even if I knew where they'd gone it wouldn't do you any good.'

I went cold. 'What do you mean?' I started to squeeze my fingers around his throat. Heraud started to choke and clawed pointlessly at my hand. I squeezed harder. Heraud's eyes bulged. He waved a hand and tried to nod his head. I relaxed my grip a little.

'Simpson put them into the computer system,' said Heraud. He started coughing and retching.

'What do you mean?'

'He had them both admitted as patients,' said Heraud, rubbing his neck.

'Why?' I asked him.

Heraud didn't look as if he wanted to answer me. Again I hit him on the side of his head with the flat of my hand. I didn't object to hurting him and I didn't even feel ashamed of myself.

'We use the computer for our drug records,' he said hoarsely.

'Go on.'

'Dr Simpson can control the details of drug dosages from London,' said Heraud. 'He sometimes changes them for patients who've been signed up for annuities.'

'Like the one you wanted my mother to sign?'

Heraud looked terrified. Courage wasn't his strong suit. 'He can increase the dosage instructions on the computer then, when the extra dose has been given he can change the records back again.'

I remembered my conversation with the policeman. It wasn't surprising that he hadn't managed to find any evidence to convict Simpson.

'So there's never any evidence to prove that the drug dosages have been changed?'

Heraud nodded.

'Don't the nurses get suspicious?'

This time Heraud shook his head. 'Deaths are so common among the elderly that no one notices.'

I must have looked disbelieving.

'Nurses and doctors expect patients to die. But no one ever checks anyway. These are old people.' Heraud shrugged. Sweat was pouring off him.

'There are no post mortems?'

He shook his head. 'Everyone just assumes they died naturally.'

'And Simpson and Lonsdale collect the annuity money?'

Heraud was trembling with fear and didn't answer.

'That's murder.'

'They are all old people,' said Heraud. 'They would have died before long anyway.'

'It's still murder.'

'It was outside my control,' said Heraud, pitifully. 'I just did what I was told.'

I felt neither contempt nor pity for this miserable man. 'Is Simpson planning to kill Barbara and Lizzie the same way?' I said. 'By using the computer to instruct nurses to give them drugs that will kill them?'

Heraud just looked at me. He didn't say anything but there was a wealth of meaning in the silence.

'I want to see their records.' I told him.

'You can't!' said Heraud. He was on his knees. 'They aren't registered here,' he said. 'We can only check on patients who are registered at this nursing home.' He was sweating so much I believed him. 'Simpson and Lonsdale are the only people who have access to all the computer records.'

I stood still. I didn't know what to do next.

I was shaken by this uncertainty when Heraud, who had seen someone behind my back, suddenly threw himself forward and yelled out for help.

I turned my head just in time to see two men in white coats run into the room. I staggered backwards a few feet as Heraud's shoulder hit me in the stomach. Acting instinctively I made a fist with my right hand and brought it crashing down on the back of Heraud's head. He collapsed onto the floor, moaning but not moving. I turned swiftly and hit the leading white coat with a left hook. I then swung wildly at the second man and missed him by half a yard.

But the miss was good enough. Seeing his two colleagues on the floor the second white coat turned and started to edge back towards the door starting to shout for more help. I was too quick for him and before he had time to shout anything intelligible I had dived, tackled him and brought him down on the hard floor. He lay groaning and still. He didn't want to fight. He probably wasn't paid to fight. Not realising that real life fights never last as long as fights in the movies I was surprised.

I left Heraud's office and headed for the front door. Two minutes later I was running as fast as my bad leg would carry me down the long driveway.

I had to get back to London.

CHAPTER TWENTY-EIGHT

I caught a fast suburban commuter train to Charles de Gaulle airport and then caught a flight to Heathrow Airport. From the airport a tube ride and a taxi got me back to my flat by early morning.

After showering and changing into clean clothes I checked my answering machine while waiting for the kettle to boil. There were two messages from my wife wanting to know if I'd got a lawyer yet, one from a friend with news of a freelance job for a magazine, two inviting me to parties and one from Lindsay.

'Hello,' she said. She introduced herself and gave the date and the time. Then there was a pause. 'I very much enjoyed seeing you again,' she said, slightly hesitantly. 'On reflection I think it was a terrible place to meet. We should have met on neutral ground – somewhere where neither of us are known.' There was another pause. 'I would like to see you again,' she said. 'Seeing you brought back some very happy memories.' There was another long, long pause.

She sounded shy, rather hesitant and more vulnerable. She sounded more like the Lindsay I used to know.

'If you like perhaps we could meet for lunch sometime? Perhaps you'd give me a call when you can?' Again there was another long pause. 'If you'd like to, of course.'

Then after another long pause the phone went down.

I turned the answering machine off, looked up Lindsay's number, picked up the phone and dialled.

Her crisp, professional voice answered. It was her answering machine.

I hesitated for a moment, opened my mouth to speak, panicked and slammed the receiver down.

I picked up the telephone again almost immediately and telephoned Michael Sunderland.

Another answering machine.

I looked at my watch. It was twenty past ten. Michael would be in court. I wondered what time the court rose for lunch. I needed to speak to him quickly.

Downstairs in the underground garage there was another note tucked under the windscreen wipers of the Bentley. I pulled it out, glanced at the signature and threw it into the nearby rubbish bin without reading it. I knew it had to be another strongly worded letter from the people who didn't like the length of my car.

The traffic was, as usual, horrendous. Baker Street was at a standstill and I turned left along Marylebone Road where the traffic was moving. I turned into Portland Place, drove past the British Broadcasting Corporation's radio studios and headed down Regent street towards Piccadilly Circus. Deciding to stick with traffic that was moving I turned up into Shaftsbury Avenue and then drove along New Oxford Street. I was heading for the Aldwych. When I got to The Strand the traffic was absolutely solid. There was nowhere to go and nowhere to park. I turned the steering wheel sharply to the left and pulled the Bentley up onto the pavement on the left hand side of the Aldwych. No one seemed to notice. The pedestrians simply circulated around the car. I locked it and ran towards the Old Bailey.

The guard at the entrance to the courts wasn't exactly helpful. I asked him to see if Terry, my contact, could spare me a few minutes. He made the telephone call reluctantly.

'The court has risen but you can't see anyone on jury service,' Terry said emphatically. He looked even more miserable than ever.

'It's a vitally important personal matter,' I explained. 'I must speak to Michael Sunderland.'

'I couldn't let you do that,' insisted Terry.

'Would you let me speak to him on the telephone?' I begged. 'That can hardly interfere with the cause of justice can it?'

Terry seemed totally disinterested.

'I'll pay for the call, of course.' I assured him, producing a small wad of ten pound notes.

111

'I'll see what I can do,' said Terry, enlivened by the sight of the notes.

A few minutes later Terry pointed me to a telephone. 'You've got two minutes.'

He didn't offer to move away.

'It's very personal,' I said, taking the telephone receiver but holding a hand over the mouthpiece. 'I'd be very grateful.'

Terry grumbled a little but moved away just out of earshot.

'Michael?'

'Yes. Who's that?'

'Mark Watson.'

'Where are you?'

'London. I'm at the law courts but they won't let me in to talk to you.'

'Where's Barbara? Is she with you? Have you seen her? Is she O.K.?'

'I think Barbara is still O.K.'

'Where is she? Where's Lizzie?'

'I don't know where either of them are. They've been moved.'

'How did you get away?' asked Michael. 'They sent me a photo of the three of you together.'

'It's a long story,' I said. 'The important thing is that the jury mustn't make a decision too quickly.'

'Why? What do you mean?' asked Michael. 'I think I'm getting them round to my view.'

'Slow it down. Just slow it down.'

Michael was confused. 'But Lonsdale wants us to find him not guilty.'

'Sshhhh. Careful.' I looked around, terrified in case anyone had heard him. 'No names.'

'It's O.K.,' said Michael. 'There's no one listening at this end. Why do you want me to slow things down?'

'Because as long as there is some uncertainty about the outcome they'll want to keep their hold over you.'

'You think that whatever happens they'll kill Barbara and Lizzie after the trial?'

'They might. It's a risk I don't want to take.'

Terry who'd been looking anxiously at his watch walked back towards me. 'Time's up!' he said. 'Sorry.'

'I'll speak to you this evening,' I said to Michael. 'Just try to keep things going for as long as you can. Keep the other jurors talking.'

CHAPTER TWENTY-NINE

The Bentley was still parked where I'd left it but an unpatriotic policeman with no respect for doctors had stuck a large square of paper to the windscreen warning me not to try driving it away. A huge yellow Denver boot clamped to the offside front wheel made such an option impractical. A traffic warden was stationed close to the car, his arms folded and a very glum look on his face.

Deciding that the Bentley would be safe enough where it was, guarded and unstealable, I walked back along the Strand towards Trafalgar Square. I was fairly confident that Lonsdale wouldn't harm Barbara or Lizzie until the jury had reached their verdict. I was equally confident that the moment the verdict had been announced – whatever it was – then Barbara and Lizzie would both die of medical accidents. Assuming that Michael could delay the jury's decision by another three hours, thereby taking the trial into another day, I would have until sometime tomorrow to come up with a method of persuading Lonsdale to set the two women free.

Violence was my first thought.

As I walked along the Strand, past the Savoy and past Charing Cross Station, I had a vision of myself bursting into Lonsdale's offices, pinning him to the floor and forcing him to tell me where Barbara and Lizzie were being held. In this fanciful scenario I then saw myself flying to Frankfurt, Nice, Geneva or Barcelona and rescuing the two women like a knight on a white charger.

There was one enormous snag with this plan.

Assuming that I could get into Lonsdale's offices and over-power his guards and pin him to the floor and force him to give

114

me the information I would then have to leave him while I flew off to perform the rescue.

What would Lonsdale do?

The moment I left the room he would telephone the nursing home in the city I was heading for and instruct them to kill Barbara and Lizzie immediately. He wouldn't even have to do that. He could just phone Simpson and get him to fix their computer controlled drug dosages. They would be dead long before I got to them.

And what if they were being held in separate nursing homes? I hadn't thought of that. What if Barbara was being held in Brussels and Lizzie was being held in Rome? It would take me over a day to rescue the two of them. Even assuming that I met no resistance in the two nursing homes.

The further I walked the more depressed I got.

To stop Lonsdale harming the two women I would have to make sure that he couldn't talk. And that would mean killing him. Tying him up wouldn't do – someone might find him and let him loose.

And even if I did kill him what about Simpson? (I realised with some surprise that I wasn't shocked to find myself thinking about murder as a possible option.) If he found out that Lonsdale was dead he would guess what was happening. And he'd immediately arrange for the two women to be killed.

By the time I reached Trafalgar Square I was in despair.

I walked up towards Charing Cross Road. The sun, which had been shining for most of the morning, had gone in and the bleak, dark clouds matched my mood.

I was walking along Oxford Street in the direction of Oxford Circus when I passed a shop selling computers. That gave me an idea. I slipped into a nearby bookshop and consulted a couple of reference books. After half an hour a plan was beginning to develop. Half running now, despite my painful leg, I went down into the Oxford Circus underground station and caught the Piccadilly Line train out to Heathrow airport, grateful that I had brought my passport with me. From Heathrow I caught the next Swiss Air flight out to Zurich.

CHAPTER THIRTY

I got back to London that evening.

Michael Sunderland and the rest of the jury had been sent to a hotel for the night because they still hadn't managed to reach a verdict. I sat in my local pub and in his absence drank a toast to him. He'd spent several days persuading the rest of the jury to ignore the prosecution's evidence and come in with a 'not guilty' verdict. Now I need him to keep stalling for time. We still needed a 'not guilty' verdict – but not yet.

Now, it was up to me. I looked at my watch. It was nine forty five. I had maybe fifteen hours to turn the tables on Lonsdale and Simpson. I pushed my empty plate to one side and drank the remainder of the lemonade I'd ordered. The food in the pub was awful but I didn't want to spend the whole evening in my flat feeling lonely and sorry for myself.

I planned to break into the nursing home at around one o'clock. I didn't dare go too soon because I needed the place to be fairly quiet. But I didn't dare go too late either because I had a lot of work to do.

I decided to go back to the flat, have a shower and get changed.

When I got in the red light on my answering machine was shining and a bright green number 1 told me that someone had called while I'd been out. I rewound the tape and played back the call while I filled the kettle.

It was Lindsay.

'I didn't mean to ring you again,' she said and then hesitated. 'But I just wondered if you'd got my message.' There was a longer pause. 'I have thought about you a lot.' There was another long pause. Then there was a 'click' as she put the telephone down.

I rang her.

'I'm glad you called,' she said. 'I'm sorry about the other evening.'

'I'm glad you called,' I said. 'I'd like to see you again.'

'What are you doing now?' she asked. 'Tonight?'

I looked at my watch. 'I've got to go out in an hour or two.'

'Can we meet?'

'Do you want to come round here?'

'I'd love to.'

I gave her the address, said goodbye and put the phone down. Then I made a phone call to Zurich to change some of the arrangements I'd made that afternoon, had a shower and looked in vain for some clean clothes.

She arrived before I had time to dress and so I slipped my dressing gown on when I heard the doorbell go.

'I'm sorry about the mess,' I apologised, waving a hand around the kitchen. 'I've been a bit busy.' I looked down at my dressing gown. 'I've just had a shower.'

She looked around and laughed.

'My wife took the best furniture. I've thrown the rest out.' I explained.

'I'm sorry,' she said.

I didn't want to talk about my wife. 'You were married, weren't you?'

'It didn't work out.' She pulled a face.

There was a long silence.

'But he kept most of the furniture,' she said, and laughed.

'They should get together,' I suggested. 'They could open up a furniture store.'

'I'm glad you rang,' said Lindsay after another long silence.

'I'm glad you rang.'

'What time do you have to go out?'

I looked at my watch. 'Not just yet.'

'Work?' she asked.

'Sort of.'

We stood and looked at one another for a long time.

'Did I tell you I found some photos of you the other day?'

'I bet I looked terrible!' she laughed. 'Embroidered jeans, tee shirt with a silly message, long straight hair.'

'You looked lovely.' I said then felt slightly uncomfortable.

It had been a long time since I'd done any courting. 'Would you like a drink?'

'Have you got any white wine?'

Sorry,' I said. 'I meant coffee, tea. I don't have anything alcoholic.'

'Your wife took the booze cabinet?'

I grinned. 'I don't drink much.'

'Tea, please, then.'

There was another long pause after I put the kettle on. I didn't know what to say. I didn't want to talk about the past. And we didn't yet have a present or a future to talk about. I knew her too well to make the sort of polite, small talk that one makes at parties. But I no longer knew her well enough for the silences to be entirely comfortable.

The kettle was behind her and to reach I had to move past her. I never got to it. I don't know who made the first move. It seemed as though we came together naturally and inevitably.

Her lips were as warm and as soft as I remembered them. Her perfume made me dizzy. Her body was fuller than I remembered and, if anything, more voluptuous. I pulled her to me and held her tight. She whispered my name and I could feel her trembling in my arms.

She whispered something in my ear.

I hadn't felt so good for a long time.

She put her hands behind my neck and pulled my head towards her. We kissed again and I crushed her soft body to me.

CHAPTER THIRTY-ONE

Lindsay was wrapped in my arms.

'I'm so glad I found you again,' she murmured.

'Me too.' I lowered my head and kissed her neck and then her shoulder.

'Do you have to go out? Can't you stay?'

I looked at my watch. It was half past eleven. 'I have to go.' I held her head and kissed her on the lips.

'How long will you be?'

'I don't know.'

'Can I stay here and wait for you?'

'Yes.' I held her tight. 'Yes, please.'

She seemed to understand that something was worrying me. She pulled back a little and frowned. 'What's the matter?' she asked. She looked concerned. 'Where have you got to go?'

I told her about Michael Sunderland. I told her about Lonsdale. I told her about Barbara. I told her about Lizzie. I told her about the nursing home in Paris. It was a relief to be able to talk to someone.

'So what are you going to do now?'

'I need to get at the computer that Simpson uses,' I explained. 'If I can't do something then they'll kill Michael Sunderland's wife and sister.'

'What will you do when you've found out where they are?'

'Try to get them out, I suppose.' I knew it wasn't going to be that easy.

'What sort of person is Lonsdale?' asked Lindsay.

'Greedy. Everything he does is for money. That's what drives him. A man I knew once said that the best way to control rich people is to threaten to turn them into poor people. So I'm going to use the computer to try to turn him into a poor person,' I said. 'It's my only hope.'

Lindsay looked at me and frowned. 'I don't understand.'

'Lonsdale and Simpson rely on the computer to control just about everything relating to their nursing homes,' I explained. 'And Heraud in Paris told me that they use it to control all their financial affairs too.'

Lindsay still looked puzzled.

'Computers are very vulnerable,' I explained. 'Worms, viruses, logic bombs, salami.'

Lindsay laughed.

'A lot of the stories I wrote for the paper were about computer fraud,' I told her.

'But what on earth is a worm?'

'It's a program designed to alter the way a computer system works, or to delete specific parts of the computer memory or to shut it down completely,' I explained. 'A good worm can cause chaos. One of the best worms was used by a computer programmer in America. He was promised a permanent position with a large bank if he successfully managed to develop a new financial package for them. One of their requirements was for an automated payroll program. He did so well,' I continued, 'that the company reneged on their promise and sacked him a couple of months after he'd finished the project. But exactly one month later the program he'd installed suddenly stopped working. And it didn't work again until the programmer had been reinstated. He'd put a code in the program which meant that the payroll program wouldn't work – and neither would anything else in the bank's computer – if his name disappeared from the list of company employees. The bank either had to get an entirely new system or else they had to rehire the programmer. It was cheaper to rehire the programmer.'

Lindsay looked impressed. 'So what's a virus? How on earth can a virus affect a computer?'

'It's not the sort of virus you're thinking of,' I told her. 'In computer language a virus is a program that instructs the computer to summon up stored files. Then the virus copies itself out onto the software. The result is absolute chaos. Programs can be ruined.'

'A logic bomb?'

'Putting a logic bomb into a computer is like lighting a time fuse. You can program software to self destruct if the bomb isn't defused. Employees often put logic bombs into computer software to protect themselves.'

'So a logic bomb is a bit like a worm?'

I nodded.

'And a salami...what on earth is a salami?'

'A programming technique designed to slice off small amounts of money without anyone noticing. The best and simplest salamis merely take the odd fractions off interest payments – and then put those fractions into the programmer's personal account. A programmer in Germany helped himself to more than a million deutschmarks in half pfennigs before anyone noticed what was happening. Individual clients of the bank where he worked never complained because they never expected to receive half a pfennig or a third of a pfennig in interest.'

'How on earth can you steal more than a million deutschmarks in half pfennigs?'

'Easy. You can do it in a couple of months. If a bank has millions of customers and they all lose half a pfennig a day.'

'I'm beginning to think that computers aren't quite as secure as they ought to be,' said Lindsay.

I laughed. 'Computers secure? Anyone who claims that information is secure when it's in a computer is either a fool or a crook.'

'But don't the police come down strongly on people who fiddle information out of computers – or who use computers to steal money?'

I shook my head. 'Most of the time the police don't even know. Banks don't like admitting that their computer systems are easy to get into so they take the losses and say nothing. And even when computer fraud is discovered it's never taken seriously.'

'Oh, I can't believe that!' said Lindsay.

'The average bank robber in America gets $20,000. If he's caught he has a 90% chance of being prosecuted and if he is convicted he's likely to get at least 5 years in prison. The average computer fraudster gets $500,000, has a very low chance of being caught, has only 15% chance of being prosecuted if he is caught and even if he is prosecuted and convicted is likely to spend no more than 5 months in prison – and an open, white collar prison at that.'

'To all that,' I went on, 'you have to add the fact that the traditional bank robber will almost certainly have to give back the loot. The computer thief salts his money away in a special account in Switzerland within minutes of stealing it. He never even has to handle the cash.'

'So, what are you going to use to get a hold over Lonsdale and Simpson?'

I shrugged. 'I'm not sure yet.'

Lindsay started to dress. 'I'm coming with you,' she said, pulling on her stockings.

'No, you're not!'

'I want to help.' She adjusted her suspender belt and fastened a stocking to it.

I shook my head. 'No!' I said firmly. I put my hands on her shoulders. 'Thank you but no!'

'I want to help.' She bent down to pick up her bra.

'They've already kidnapped another woman because of me,' I said. 'I should have never allowed Michael's sister to help me.'

'I can look after myself,' Lindsay said, fastening her bra.

'Not with these people you can't.' I bent my head and kissed her. I held her head a few inches from mine. 'Please!' I begged. 'Stay here.'

'But I want to help you.'

'You can,' I promised. 'If I'm not back by eight tomorrow morning come round to Lonsdale's nursing home with a camera crew. Demand to see Lonsdale. Make a fuss.'

She stared at me for a long time without saying anything. 'I don't want to lose you again,' she said softly.

'You won't,' I promised. I paused. 'There is one other thing you could do for me. I left my car parked in the Aldwych. It was clamped. You can't miss it.'

Lindsay smiled and held out her hand. 'Keys.'

I found the keys and gave them to her.

'What sort is it?'

'An old Bentley. It's parked on the pavement opposite Bush House.'

Lindsay looked impressed. 'I've never driven a Bentley before,' she said. 'Where do I put it when I've liberated it?'

'There's an underground garage here.'

'Is your life always this complicated?'

I grinned.

She was fully dressed now. She stood on tiptoe and kissed me full on the lips.

CHAPTER THIRTY-TWO

Lonsdale's London nursing home looked quiet and peaceful. I stood on the other side of the road for a few minutes and stared at it. A cab had dropped me off five minutes earlier.

Eventually, I had to make a move. Standing on the pavement wasn't going to change anything.

During my years as an investigative reporter I've learned that the best way to get into somewhere that you're not supposed to be is to march in confidently. If you walk in looking nervous or diffident then someone will pounce on you and throw you out. If you walk in looking as though you don't only own the place but are also planning wholesale redundancies then everyone will disappear into the woodwork and leave you well alone.

I marched into the nursing home, said 'Good evening!' to the uniformed guard on duty at the door and without hesitating turned left out of the reception area. The corridor I found myself in contained a number of doors marked 'Administration', 'Secretaries' and 'Personnel'. I chose the door marked 'Secretaries' and tried the doorknob. It opened.

Inside the office I went straight to the nearest desk. I knew exactly what I was looking for. I found the list of telephone extension numbers taped onto the wall by the side of the desk. Lonsdale's extension was numbered 307.

I dialled 307, put the receiver down on the desk and slipped out into the corridor. I stood still for a few seconds, listening carefully to see if I could hear a telephone ringing. Nothing. I went to the end of the corridor, pushed open a heavy firedoor and climbed the emergency stairs to the first floor.

This floor turned out to be occupied by patients. I decided

that Lonsdale's office was either going to be in the reception area on the ground floor or else on the top floor.

I decided to try the rest of the ground floor first. I didn't want to go back downstairs and cross the reception area in front of the duty guard so I walked the full length of the first floor corridor and then descended the emergency stairs at the other end. Less than a minute later I found myself in the right hand half of the ground floor corridor.

There was a telephone ringing behind the first door I came to. The door had no name on it; just a black and gold plastic sign saying 'Private'. Unless someone else was getting late night telephone calls this had to be Lonsdale's office.

I opened the door with a thin strip of celluloid that I took out of my jacket pocket. Burglars in films always use credit cards to open doors but these days credit cards are too thick, too inflexible and contain too much embossing. A man who's now serving five years for industrial espionage gave me that valuable piece of information and gave me the piece of celluloid to use.

I shut the door behind me and turned on the light. That was another useful trick I'd learned from the industrial espionage expert.

'Wander around at night with a torch and it looks suspicious,' he'd said. 'But if you turn on a main light no one is going to be suspicious. They'll just assume that either someone is working late or else some lazy sod has left a light on.' Too late I wondered how he'd got caught if he'd been so damned clever.

I lifted Lonsdale's telephone and then put the receiver down on his desk so that it wouldn't keep on ringing. The computer terminal that I'd come to see was sitting in the middle of Lonsdale's expensive executive desk.

I sat down, leant forward and switched on the computer. Almost instantaneously the screen lit up. The single word CODE appeared in the middle of the screen.

I had known that in order to hack my way into the system I would need at least one codeword but that didn't worry me as much as it perhaps should have done. Theoretically computer code words should provide an impenetrable barrier; they should protect the contents of a computer program from any unauthorised eyes. But, like all other aspects of computer technology, the weak link is always the human operator. Most people who have to create private and confidential codewords for their computers either use words or collections of figures or letters that mean something to them – and then write their codewords down and hide them somewhere.

I took from my jacket pocket the crumpled sheet of paper that contained the information I'd collected about Lonsdale and Simpson when I'd visited the Oxford Street bookshop.

For twenty minutes I tried everything I could think of that might prove to be the entry code to Lonsdale's computer. I tried his first name, his initials, his birthday, his astrological sign and every combination of these things that I could think of.

Nothing.

I decided to see if Lonsdale had written anything down. I opened the top drawer of his desk. It contained the usual collection of papers and stationery; old pens, a ruler, refill pages for a Filofax, a few envelopes addressed in a woman's handwriting and an old diary.

The diary, a pocket appointments diary for last year, looked most promising. I opened and found the section in which Lonsdale had listed telephone numbers of friends and acquaintances. And I struck gold.

At the bottom of the first page there were three numbers listed that were clearly not telephone numbers. Each consisted of just four numerals. Lonsdale had written a Christian name by the side of each of these numbers in an attempt to make them look like telephone numbers. His imagination had, however, not worked overtime. The names he had chosen were Tom, Dick and Harry. My guess was that two of these number codes were PIN numbers for bank cards. I was hoping that the third number code would be the entry to Lonsdale's computer.

It was 'Harry' who opened up Lonsdale's business and financial world to me. It was 'Harry' who betrayed him.

The programme that Lonsdale used to keep track of his empire was well written and easy to use.

First, I wanted to know that Barbara and Lizzie were still alive and well. I didn't believe that with the jury still out Lonsdale would have risked harming either of them. He would want to be able to carry on providing Michael with photographs and tapes of his wife.

I knew that neither Lonsdale nor Simpson would have been stupid enough to register Barbara or Lizzie under their real names but I knew the date on which they had both been moved from Paris and it didn't take me long to find them. All I had to do was to find women of approximately the right age who had been admitted on the right date and who weren't recorded as having any notifiable next of kin.

I traced one of them to a nursing home in Madrid and the other to a nursing home in Brussels. I wasn't sure which of them was where. Both had been admitted for general nursing care and both had been described as British holidaymakers who had collapsed while away from home. Neither of them had so far been prescribed any drug therapy. My guess was that the moment the trial was over Simpson would slip in a prescription for something common but potentially deadly and untraceable – an overdose of insulin or digoxin, for example. Then the drug instructions would be removed from the computer and if anyone ever proved that the women had been given drugs a nurse would be left to take the blame for just another regrettable mistake. No one would be likely to spot a link between an accidental death in Brussels and an accidental death in Madrid.

I looked at my watch. I'd been in the London nursing home for just under an hour and I'd been in Lonsdale's office for fifty minutes. I thought of Barbara and Lizzie, lying frightened and alone in nursing home beds. I thought of Lindsay. She was probably home by now. My home. In my bed. I tried not to think of her. I thought of Michael. He must be close to breaking point by now. I still had a lot to do.

I bent over the computer and went back to work.

CHAPTER THIRTY-THREE

The receptionist was busy with her nails. Her tongue peeped out between her lips as she concentrated. She finished painting the nail on the little finger of her left hand and held it at arm's length to examine her work. She blew on the nails a couple of times and then shook her fingers gently. Satisfied, she carefully transferred the polish brush from her right hand to her left hand. She gripped it tightly but carefully between her thumb and forefinger so as not to smudge the polish that she had already applied. Then she started on the nails of her right hand.

I stood and watched her. It took another two minutes for her to paint each of the nails on her right hand. Then she carefully screwed the cap back on the bottle of bright red nail varnish, waved both hands in the air a few times and looked up. She seemed genuinely surprised to see me standing there. She raised a neatly manicured eyebrow.

'I've come to see Dr Simpson.'

The receptionist picked up the grey telephone in front of her and used a pencil to dial a three figure number. She held the telephone cautiously, taking care not to smudge her nails. It made her look as though she found the telephone offensive or distasteful in some way. She spoke for a moment, listened carefully and then dropped the telephone back onto its rest.

'He's got someone with him,' she said. 'You'll have to wait.' She nodded towards a pair of low, black, imitation leather chairs on the other side of the narrow reception area. A low glass topped coffee table stood in front of the two chairs. Upon it lay a pile of magazines.

I yawned and had to struggle hard to stay awake. I'd got back to my flat at just after 6.30 am. The keys to the Bentley had been on the kitchen table together with the receipt from the police. Lindsay had been fast asleep in bed. I had bent over her, moved her hair back off her face and kissed her forehead. She had looked beautiful and innocent.

Then I'd gone back into the kitchen and left a message on Michael's answering machine asking him to find people who could fly out to Madrid and Brussels and wait for Barbara and Lizzie to be released.

'Your parents and Barbara's parents would be best,' I'd said. 'Just get them to fly out there now. Get them to book into big, central, easy-to-find hotels and to ring me at home and let me know where they're staying. They can leave the numbers on my answering machine.'

After that I'd gone to bed. But I hadn't slept.

*　　*　　*

'Dr Simpson will see you now.'

I looked up. The receptionist was smiling at me. At least she was trying to smile. Sadly, the effort merely made her look rather simple-minded. She needed lessons from Lindsay. Lindsay had a wonderful smile. Lindsay had a wonderful everything.

I followed the receptionist's pointed finger and entered Simpson's office. It was lavishly and expensively furnished.

I hadn't seen Simpson in good light before and could only remember his voice from our previous encounters. He wore a plain, light grey, three piece suit with a pink shirt. His tie was red and despite the waistcoat he wore a gold tie pin. A red handkerchief which matched the tie blossomed from his breast pocket. He had three inches of white cuff showing and each cuff was fastened with embossed gold cufflinks. I got the impression that Simpson thought he looked elegant.

He looked startled when he saw me and his body language spoke volumes. He pushed his chair back so that he could get as far away from me as possible. He glanced nervously at the door as though trying to decide if he could get past me and escape.

'I want you to release Barbara and Lizzie Sunderland,' I said. I wanted to kill him. But I needed him alive so I smiled at him as I spoke. I read somewhere that if you smile at people they're much more inclined to like you.

Simpson laughed. A hollow, empty, frightened laugh.

'What on earth are you talking about?' he asked me, when

he'd recovered his composure. It didn't take long. He wasn't a man who allowed himself to get carried away by emotion.

I looked at my watch. 'The jury at the Old Bailey should be delivering their verdict soon,' I said. 'My information is that your friend Lonsdale stands a very good chance of being acquitted.' I sat on the edge of his desk. 'Would you do me a favour?' I asked him. 'Just so that we can both save time?'

Simpson looked at me. He didn't look like a man who liked doing favours for people.

'It won't take you a moment,' I assured him. 'And it won't cost you anything.'

'What?' he asked, suspiciously.

'Check your company bank balance.'

Without saying anything Simpson played the computer keyboard in front of him. It's probably an exaggeration to say that he turned white. But he got pretty close to it. Then, when he'd gone about as white as seemed possible, his face rapidly began to regain its colour. Instead of stopping at pink it went straight through to red. He looked at me and then looked back at the computer screen. He opened a drawer in his desk and took out a foil strip containing a dozen red capsules. He pushed one of the capsules free from the foil, picked a glass of water up off his desk and swallowed the capsule.

'What sort of trick is this?'

'It isn't a trick,' I assured him.

'I don't know what the hell you think you're doing,' he said, 'but you won't get away with it.' He tried to look fierce but it was probably about as convincing as his considerate and caring, bedside manner look.

I just smiled at him.

'There's £25 million missing.' He paused. 'Do you know where it is? Have you stolen it?' He was getting quite belligerent now that he realised that money was involved.

'Maybe you should call the police.'

He didn't seem very enthusiastic about that option.

'It hasn't been stolen,' I told him. 'I'm not a thief. It's just been moved.'

'Where to? Where have you moved it?' He wasn't at all happy.

'It's very safe,' I told him. 'I'll tell you exactly where it is when Barbara and Lizzie Sunderland are safe.'

Simpson stared at the computer screen. He hammered a few keys.

'You won't find it,' I told him.

Simpson reached for a telephone. 'I've got people who'll persuade you to tell me what you've done with it.'

'You may have people who can hurt me or even kill me,' I agreed. 'But that won't help you a lot. No one can get at the money without me – and you need me in good health.'

Simpson pulled his hand away from the telephone. 'I'll talk to Jerry Lonsdale,' he said. 'I can't do anything without him. He'll arrange for Barbara and...,' he paused. 'What did you say her name was?'

'Lizzie.'

'And Lizzie to be released.' He spoke quietly as though afraid of being overheard. He seemed to think that I would trust him.

'I want them released now,' I said.

'I can't do anything until I see Jerry.'

'There's something else you should know,' I said. 'Ring the Suisse Credit International in Berne. Ask for a statement of what's in your personal account.'

Simpson looked at me as if I'd gone mad. 'I haven't got a bank account in Switzerland,' he insisted.

'Ring them.' I said. And I gave him the number of his personal, private account and the telephone number of the bank. A personal, private account he didn't know he had.

I waited while he rang the bank and then spoke to one of the Swiss cashiers. Then he slammed down the phone.

'What the hell have you done?' he demanded.

I didn't answer.

'What have you done?' he screamed. He was standing now.

'I wonder what Jerry will say when he finds out that all his money is in a private account in your name?' I stood up and left him. On my way out I passed the receptionist. 'When Mr Lonsdale comes in,' I said, 'would you give him a message?'

As I spoke to the receptionist Simpson rushed past me. I looked at my watch. 'There's a plane to Zurich in ninety minutes,' I told him. 'You should just catch it. British Airways.'

131

Simpson glowered at me. 'I've got to go to Switzerland,' he said to the receptionist. And ran out.

The receptionist watched him go and then turned back to me. 'We're not expecting Mr Lonsdale in today,' she said. 'He's been away on business for a while.'

'Oh, I think he'll be back today,' I told her. 'And when he comes in would you ask him to ring me?' I reached over, took a pen from the holder on her desk and scribbled my telephone number on the jotter pad in front of her. 'He can reach me there,' I told her.

'May I ask what it's about?' asked the receptionist.

'Just tell him that it's about his money.'

The receptionist looked puzzled.

'Just ask Mr Lonsdale to check his company bank account,' I told her. 'And then if he wants to know where his money has gone get him to give me a ring.'

CHAPTER THIRTY-FOUR

Lindsay poured us both fresh mugs of coffee before she sat down.

'How long have you been a vegetarian?'

I shrugged. 'I can't remember. A few years.'

'Why?'

'Who wants to eat dead animals?'

She laughed.

I tasted the scrambled egg. It was perfect: light and frothy.

'I still don't understand,' she said, sipping at her coffee. It was still too hot to drink. 'What did you do with their money? How could you get into their bank account?'

I tasted one of the potato cakes. It was perfect; crisp on the outside and soft inside. 'If you've got as much money as Lonsdale and Simpson you don't move your money around in sacks. You don't use armoured cars every time you want to adjust your investments. You don't even use cheques or bankers' drafts.'

Lindsay put her mug down.

'Big companies move their money about electronically. Every day in London the Foreign Exchange markets transfer over $200 billion using a system called Electronic Fund Transfer.'

'And Lonsdale is in that league?'

I nodded. 'He has nursing homes in just about every country in Europe. That means that he has money coming in in God knows how many different currencies – and that's not counting the money he handles for the Las Vegas people who are laundering their spare cash. You can make – or lose – a fortune by making sure that your funds are in the right currency at the right time – or, just as important, not in the wrong currency at the wrong time.'

'So how does Electronic whatever you call it work?'

'It's all done with satellites. The transactions are very fast and once they're completed there is no calling them back. The whole thing is done with computers, of course. It's a sort of grown-up version of the sort of electronic transfer they're using in shops when you buy a packet of sugar in the supermarket and your bank account is debited instantly and automatically.'

'And you've used the Electronic transfer system to steal all their money?'

'I haven't stolen it. I've just put it somewhere safe for a while so that I've got something to bargain with.'

'But if it's that easy why isn't it happening all the time?'

'It is. Computer crime is the fastest growing industry in the world. It makes ordinary crime look what it is – cheap, crude and amateurish. Today's big crooks are heavily into computer theft.'

'It sounds absurdly easy.'

'Once you have access to a company's main computer you can do almost anything,' I pointed out.

'And Lonsdale and Simpson can't get at their money?'

'No.'

'Isn't there a chance that they might manage to find out where you've put it? After all you found out where they'd hidden Barbara and Lizzie.'

'They weren't expecting anyone to go looking for Barbara and Lizzie through the computer,' I said. 'Like a lot of people who use computers they assume that everyone else is still in the dark ages.'

'How much of it have you moved?'

'Every penny. £25 million from their company account.'

'Wow!' Lindsay sucked in her breath.

*   *   *

The two telephone calls I was waiting for came within five minutes of each another.

The first call came from Michael.

'Not guilty!' he said breathlessly. 'We found him not guilty. Is there any news? What happens now?'

I could hear lots of noise in the background. 'What's going on?'

'I'm in a pay phone in the lobby. The place is full of reporters. I tried to speak to Lonsdale but I couldn't.'

'Where is he now?'

'He rushed off in a car.'

'Go back to your flat,' I told him. 'Get there as fast as you can. There are some instructions on your answering machine. Do it. O.K?'

'O.K.'

'I'll ring you and let you know what's happening. If it isn't me who calls it'll be someone called Lindsay.'

'O.K.' said Michael.

'I'll have to go now,' I told him. 'I'm expecting a call from Lonsdale.'

Michael started to ask more questions. I didn't blame him but I didn't have time to answer them.

'I'm sorry, Michael,' I said. 'Please go home. I must go.' I put the telephone down.

Less than thirty seconds later it rang again.

'I have Mr Lonsdale for you,' said a very female voice.

I waited. For a few seconds I listened to a few bars of something by Mozart. Then a gruff, very matter of fact voice came onto the line.

'Where have you put my money you little bastard?'

'It's safe.'

'I want it back. Now.'

'You can have it back when Michael Sunderland gets his wife and sister back.'

'I don't know what you're talking about,' said Lonsdale instantly.

I put the phone down.

Lindsay looked at me in horror. 'What's happened?' she asked. She spoke in a whisper.

I felt cold inside. But I smiled at her and held my hand suspended above the telephone, making it clear that I was waiting for it to ring. Lonsdale had to ring back. And I had to make him realise that I was serious. He had a reputation for being a tough negotiator.

The phone rang.

I let it ring ten times and then I picked it up. I was sweating heavily.

'Did you put the phone down on me?' shouted Lonsdale. 'No one puts the phone down on me.'

'You can have your money back when Michael Sunderland gets his wife and sister back,' I repeated. 'In good health.'

There was a long, long silence.

'We'd better meet,' he said at last. 'Come to my office. You know where it is.'

'No,' I said. 'We'll meet in the Long Room of the pavilion at Lord's,' I told him. 'In fifteen minutes time.'

'What the hell...?'

'You're still a member of the M.C.C. aren't you?'

The M.C.C. – the Marylebone Cricket Club – is the most exclusive cricket club in the world. I'd seen that he was a member when I'd been checking his personal details in an attempt to find information that might help me find a key word or abbreviation for his computer code.

'Yes...but...!'

'I'm a member too,' I said. 'Middlesex and Surrey are playing. I'll meet you in the Long Room.'

For the second time I put the telephone down on Jerry Lonsdale.

'What was all that about?' asked Lindsay. 'Lord's is a cricket ground, isn't it? Why there?'

'Because the pavilion will be crowded today,' I explained. 'It's a big London match. And I don't trust Lonsdale.' I went through into the bedroom, opened my wardrobe and pulled out my sports jacket. 'Besides,' I went on, 'the pavilion at Lord's is one of the most difficult places to get into in the country.' I snatched a tie from the rack. Lord's is an old-fashioned place and no one gets in unless they're wearing a jacket and tie. 'Both Lonsdale and I are members,' I explained. 'But I doubt if any of his heavies are members – so he'll have to meet me alone!'

CHAPTER THIRTY-FIVE

I didn't know whether Lonsdale would recognise me. But I knew I wouldn't have any difficulty in recognising him. I sat on one of the old-fashioned chairs in the Long Room and tried to look calmer than I felt.

There are several entrances to the Long Room. The one at the front leads directly onto the steps from the pavilion to the playing area. I didn't think he'd come that way. The two at each end of the back wall lead into the two entrance hallways.

Lonsdale burst through the right hand door less than five minutes after I'd arrived. He was wearing a charcoal-grey three piece suit, a white shirt and a dark blue tie. His face was flushed and he was sweating slightly. He stood no more than six feet away from where I was sitting and looked around, his eyes restless.

'Looking for me?' I asked him quietly.

He glared at me.

'Let's go into the bar.' The bar is one of the few places within the pavilion where talking is allowed. It would, I knew, be quiet but not empty. No bar at Lord's is ever empty when there is a match on.

I got up and led the way into the bar. Lonsdale followed me.

'Do you want a drink?' I asked him.

'I want my money!' he hissed. 'What the hell's going on?'

'Your money is safe,' I assured him. 'Well, relatively safe.'

'I know all about your fun and games,' said Lonsdale. He moved so close that I could smell garlic on his breath. 'If I lose so much as a quid you're dead.' He waved a fist under my nose. Nearby, two members looked startled and moved away. I was glad I'd met him in the pavilion and not in his office.

Outside there was quiet applause. It sounded as though someone had probably scored a single.

'Have you noticed how you can tell what's going on by the applause?'

Lonsdale looked at me as if I'd gone mad.

'The level of the applause tells you everything,' I said. 'A blind fellow I know can keep score just by listening to the clapping.'

Lonsdale just stared at me.

'Personally, I find it impossible to differentiate between the applause for a maiden over and the applause for a shot that gets two runs,' I confessed.

'Forget the bloody cricketing anecdotes,' snarled Lonsdale, sounding more like a cheap villain than an expensive one. 'Where have you put my money?'

'You can have your money back,' I promised him. 'Just as soon as Barbara and Lizzie Sunderland are released.'

Lonsdale pulled a white handkerchief from his trouser pocket and wiped his face. When he'd finished the handkerchief looked damp but his face was still moist.

'What's any of this got to do with you?' Lonsdale asked. 'You're a journalist aren't you?'

'I was.'

'Oh yes. You were fired weren't you?' For the first time Lonsdale came close to smiling. I thought that he was probably the sort of person who only ever gets real pleasure out of other people's discomfort or bad fortune.

I nodded.

'How much is Sunderland paying you?'

'He's covering my expenses.'

Lonsdale laughed. 'You must be a good friend of his to go to all this trouble.'

'I hardly know him.'

'Then what the devil are you mixed up in this for?'

I shrugged. 'Because he asked me to help.'

'I'll pay you ten grand to tell me where you've put my money.'

'Ten grand?'

'Cash,' nodded Lonsdale. 'And I'll forget how aggravating you've been.'

'That's not very much.'

'How much do you want?' he asked, sneering. He clearly felt more comfortable now that he thought we'd started haggling over money.

'I've told you what I want,' I said. 'Barbara and Lizzie Sunderland.'

Lonsdale stared at me for a long moment and then walked across to the bar and ordered a large whisky. He didn't ask me if I wanted a drink. A few moments later he returned, sipping his drink.

'Can I trust them?' he asked me.

'Trust who to do what?' I knew who he meant. And I knew what he was worried about.

'Keep quiet,' he said. 'I don't like people talking about me. It makes me nervous.' He took a large gulp out of the whisky and stared straight at me.

'I'm sure you can trust them,' I assured him. 'They'll want to forget all about this.'

Lonsdale stared at me again. He seemed to be able to go for ever without blinking. 'O.K.', he said at last. 'You'd better be right.'

'We can do it all from here,' I said. 'There are phones upstairs.'

Lonsdale thought for a moment and then nodded. He emptied his glass and put it back on the bar. Then we walked up to the balcony.

'What now?' he asked.

'You ring and arrange for Barbara and Lizzie to be freed,' I told him. 'I'll give you the names of the hotels in Madrid and Brussels where I want them delivering.'

'What about my money?'

'I'll tell you where it is when I know that Barbara and Lizzie are free.'

Lonsdale stared at me. 'Why should I trust you?'

'Because I'll never trust you so if we're going to do business it has to be this way.'

Lonsdale actually grinned. 'O.K.' He walked into one of the wooden cubicles, picked up a phone and started dialling. I went into the next cubicle, picked up the phone and started dialling too. First, I rang Michael Sunderland and told him what was

139

happening. He told me the names of the hotels where his and Barbara's parents would be. I gave him a number to ring the moment he heard that Barbara and Lizzie were both safe. Then I told him that Lindsay would be calling at his flat.

'Have you still got some cash left from the sale of your car?'

'Yes.'

When Lindsay arrives do what she says.'

Silence.

'Promise?'

'O.K.'

I put the phone down and told Lonsdale the names of the two hotels. Then I rang Lindsay.

'Are you O.K?' she asked, when she heard my voice. She sounded worried. It felt good. It was a long time since anyone had worried about me.

'Fine,' I assured her. 'I'm still at Lord's. I'll have to stay here for a while.' Outside on the playing area something exciting had happened. The small crowd was being very noisy.

'Can I do anything to help?' she asked me.

'Call a taxi,' I told her. 'Go and get your passport and throw a few things into an overnight bag then go round to Michael Sunderland's flat.' I gave her the address. 'Get him to do the same. As soon as he's heard that Barbara and Lizzie are safe go straight to Heathrow and book yourselves onto a flight either to Madrid or Brussels. It doesn't matter where you go as long as you catch the earliest possible flight.'

'Are you coming?'

'Later,' I promised.

'We're presumably going to pick up Barbara and Lizzie?'

'Yes. When you've picked up one go and get the other.'

'What about Michael and Barbara's parents?'

'Thank them very much and ask them to come straight home.'

'So Michael and I end up in Brussels or Madrid with both Barbara and Lizzie. What then?'

'Go to the nearest travel agency and book yourself a holiday for four. Michael should have enough money.'

'Where to?'

I thought for a moment. I was sweating and worried in case Lonsdale could hear me. I wasn't even certain that he didn't have the flat phone bugged. 'Somewhere that they sell straw-berry ice cream.'

There was silence and for a moment I thought that she didn't remember. Then I heard her laughing quietly and I knew that she did and I knew that it was all going to be all right.

'Where will you be?' she asked.

'I've got a few things to sort out. Then I'll join you.'

'Please be careful.'

'I will. Now go. Take care. And go quickly.'

Lindsay blew me a kiss. 'Please take care,' she whispered.

'I will,' I promised. I blew her a kiss back and then I put the telephone down.

CHAPTER THIRTY-SIX

I wedged the telephone kiosk door open and Lonsdale and I sat on the balcony at Lord's and waited for Michael to ring me back. Side by side but not together we watched the cricket. It was the third day of a championship match and the two sides seemed to have settled for a draw. Middlesex had scored 376 in a first innings which had lasted for the whole of the first day and part of the second day. Surrey had been dismissed for 175 in their first innings and were now 101 without loss in their second innings.

'I can't stand this bloody game,' moaned Lonsdale impatiently looking at his watch for the umpteenth time. 'When's this call of yours going to come through?'

'Why are you a member if you hate cricket?' I asked him, genuinely puzzled.

He looked at me as though trying to decide whether I was being facetious, naive and innocent or simply stupid. He must have decided that I was innocent for he waved a hand around the balcony, pointing indiscriminately to the other members, most of whom seemed to be half asleep. 'Between them this lot run just about every bank, stock broking firm and other financial institution in the country.'

I looked around. It was hard to believe but I suspected he was right.

'I've done more business here than anywhere else I can think of,' he boasted. 'People trust each other here. Bastards who wouldn't give me two minutes of their precious time if I tried to make an appointment to see them will do a deal with me here because I become one of them.'

One of the Surrey batsmen hit the ball straight back over the bowler's head. The ball bounced a yard inside the boundary fence underneath us and the umpire signalled four runs to the scorers. The crowd clapped with politely restrained enthusiasm. An old man sitting a few yards away from us clapped without opening his eyes.

* * *

It was two hours before I heard the telephone behind me ringing. Lonsdale, who could no longer sit still had been pacing up and down in the corridor alongside the telephones. He rushed forward to fetch me but I was already on my feet.

'They're both O.K!' said Michael. He was crying as he talked. 'I spoke to both of them.'

'Good! Is Lindsay there?'

'Yes. She's got a taxi waiting downstairs. It's been there for hours.'

'Great. Do what she says.'

'Why can't Barbara and Lizzie just come back home?'

'Please!' I said. 'Trust me. Do what Lindsay says. It isn't quite over yet.' I paused. 'Have you got money?'

'Yes.'

'Good. Take it with you.'

'O.K. Lindsay wants to speak to you.'

As I waited for Lindsay to come on the line I turned so that I could see out of the telephone box. Lonsdale was standing about a few feet away from me; his eyes were glued on my face and I guessed that he was trying to read my lips. I didn't mind.

'Are you all right?' It was Lindsay.

'Yes. You?'

'Yes.' A pause. 'Please take care.'

'I will.'

'Is there anything else I can do?'

'No.'

'How long will you be?'

'I don't know. Not long.'

She blew me a kiss. I blew her one back.

'Go!' I said. I didn't want her to go. I wanted to talk to her for ever. More than that I wanted to be with her. To hold her.

'All right,' I heard her whisper. She said something else that I didn't catch and then she put the phone down.

I turned and pushed the booth door open.

'Well?' said Lonsdale.

143

'Your money is in Switzerland,' I told him. 'In an account at the Suisse Credit International in Berne.'

'Number?'

I told him. 'The account is in your partner's name.' I said. He just stared at me.

'Your partner. Simpson. The account is in his name.'

Lonsdale looked at me disbelievingly.

'Ring them if you don't believe me,' I suggested. I took a notebook out of my pocket, wrote a telephone number on a blank page, tore out the page and handed it to him. 'That's the number of the bank in Berne. Just ask if a Dr Simpson has recently opened an account there.'

Lonsdale looked at the number as though expecting it to do something.

'You'll have to get the code for Switzerland from the international operator,' I said. 'I've forgotten it.'

Lonsdale rang the operator. Minutes later he was through to the bank in Berne.

'I'm a colleague of Dr Simpson,' said Lonsdale. 'I arranged to fly out and meet him at the branch that has his account but I can't remember whether he said it was Berne or Basle.' He spoke in English, assuming that the bank's employee would understand him, and lied fluently. He gave them the number of Simpson's account.

I heard the person at the other end of the line ask Lonsdale to wait for a moment. Then, seconds later, he came back onto the line.

'Dr Simpson has an account here with us in Berne,' said the voice in clipped and precise English.

'Thank you,' said Lonsdale. He slammed the phone down and stormed out of the booth white with fury.

'What is going on?' he yelled. A couple of members twenty yards away turned and glared at us.

I shrugged.

'Are you and Simpson in this together?'

I didn't answer him directly. 'Maybe he was worried about what would happen if the jury found against you this morning,' I suggested. 'Maybe he wanted to protect your money for you in case the police came looking for it.'

'Where is he now?'

I shrugged. My shoulders were getting more exercise than they'd had for some time. 'He said he was going to Switzerland.'

Lonsdale moved forwards and grabbed my jacket by the lapels. He had to stand on tiptoes to do it.

'You promised to return my money to me,' he said.

'I promised to tell you where it was,' I corrected him. 'I've told you.' Gently but firmly I prised his fingers off my jacket.

'I don't believe you,' he said, stepping back a pace. 'I don't believe you.' He was filled with fury.

'If you don't believe me try ringing Simpson,' I suggested. 'See if he's there. Or ask his secretary where he's gone.'

Lonsdale opened the door to the telephone booth he'd used before and dialled Simpson's number. Less than two minutes later he slammed the phone down. He pushed the door open violently with his foot and stepped out of the booth.

'The bastard!' he muttered, scowling. He looked at me. 'Are you sure that you're not in this with him?'

I laughed at him. 'Me?' I said. 'Do a deal with Simpson? Do me a favour.'

'The bloody receptionist says he went to Switzerland earlier this morning,' said Lonsdale.

'When?'

'This morning. I don't know exactly when.'

I looked at my watch. 'Aren't you going after him?'

'What for?'

'If he takes the money out of Switzerland and goes to South America you'll never find him,' I explained. 'You can still buy an awful lot of obscurity for £25 million.'

Lonsdale stabbed a finger on my chest. 'You're coming with me.'

'Why?' I asked, even though it had been what I'd expected.

'First,' he said, mimicking the way I'd spoken to him earlier, 'because I don't trust you an inch. And second because if you don't I'll make another call and organise some excitement in Brussels and Madrid.' He glared at me.

I shrugged. 'If you really want my company,' I said. 'Then of course I'll come.'

For the first time I felt that I was beginning to control what was happening.

CHAPTER THIRTY-SEVEN

Lonsdale's chauffeur was waiting outside the main Grace Gates with his Rolls Royce Silver Spirit parked on double yellow lines.

'Heathrow,' snarled Lonsdale climbing into the car. 'Fast.' I followed him into the car. He lifted a lid on the back seat arm rest and removed a telephone. He pressed one of the buttons on the phone. The telephone automatically dialled a number stored in its memory.

'Put Jeffrey on,' said Lonsdale to the person who answered. He waited a few moments, impatiently tapping the fingers of his spare hand on his knee. 'Jeffrey? Bring Jed and meet me at Heathrow.'

After a pause someone, presumably Jeffrey, said something at the other end.

'How should I know? Whatever terminal handles the flights to Switzerland.'

Jeffrey said something else.

'Get Diane to ring and fix up tickets for Berne for us.'

Again Jeffrey said something that I didn't hear.

'No.' said Lonsdale flatly. 'Four. And I want them now.' He slammed the phone down and glowered at me as though he blamed me for everything which was, I suppose, fair enough.

As we drove out of the tunnel and up the approach road to Heathrow airport Lonsdale's telephone rang. It was Jeffrey ringing to tell Lonsdale where he and Jed were. They must have driven fast to have beaten us to the airport. Lonsdale told his chauffeur to go to the same terminal.

We met them by the British Airways ticket counter. Jed was an inch or two taller than me which made him about six foot five and a good three stones heavier which made him around

250 pounds. He wore a loud, checked suit and looked very like a large bookie. He was in his mid-thirties and judging by his nose and ears had either been a boxer at some stage in his career or else he had had a lot of unfortunate accidents. He stank of a particularly cheap and nasty aftershave. Jeffrey was a foot shorter and 100 pounds lighter. He wore a cream suit, tan shoes, a cream shirt and a plain green tie. He looked as though he spent a fortune at the hairdressers and was probably the first man I'd ever met who spent money having his nails manicured. He looked like a yuppie and I wasn't surprised to see that he was carrying a portable telephone and a black attaché case.

'Keep an eye on him,' said Lonsdale to Jed, nodding in my direction. 'I don't want him going anywhere that I don't go.'

Jed, who didn't look too bright, nodded and turned so that he could keep both eyes on me. I smiled back at him. I'd seen bigger, harder looking men but they'd all been carved out of stone and standing on plinths.

'Problem with the tickets,' said Jeffrey apologetically. 'No one seems to fly direct to Berne.'

Lonsdale glowered at him as though it was his fault.

'But don't worry!' said Jeffrey, holding up a calming hand. 'Diane got us four business class tickets into Zurich and I've arranged for a limo to meet us at the airport. It's only an hour or so to Berne by car.'

Lonsdale grunted.

'We've got to go straight through,' said Jeffrey. 'The plane is already boarding.'

'He's good isn't he?' I said to Lonsdale, nodding towards Jeffrey. 'Does he take dictation?'

'He's got better prospects than you have,' growled Lonsdale. Jed moved a little closer and I caught a strong whiff of his aftershave. It made me feel sick. Body odour would have been better.

The four of us were moving rapidly towards the customs barrier when I caught sight of Lindsay and Michael. Lindsay was holding Michael's arm and pointing in my direction.

I raised my hand to my face and brushed a few strands of hair out of my eyes. Then, having made sure that none of my three companions was watching me I held a finger to my lips.

Lindsay looked worried and I was frightened that she was going to do or say something.

I tapped my finger against my lips and nodded slightly to try and tell her that everything was all right.

I saw Michael lean close to Lindsay to tell her something. I guessed that he was probably telling her who Lonsdale was.

Desperate that one of them would say something I turned as we started to go through the customs barrier and tried to push Jed ahead of me. He wasn't having that. He didn't want to go anywhere ahead of me. I laughed and punched him lightly on the arm and then moved ahead of him. I wanted Lindsay and Michael to realise that I was travelling of my own free will. I desperately wanted them to get Barbara and Lizzie somewhere safe before Lonsdale stopped worrying about his money for long enough to start thinking about revenge. I reckoned it was going to take Lindsay and Michael at least twelve hours – and probably twenty four – to get Lizzie and Barbara together and to then fly off to their package holiday in the sun.

Both Lindsay and Michael looked worried but they both did what I wanted them to do: nothing. Michael buried his face in a magazine and Lindsay peered over his shoulder and feigned interest in whatever it was that he was studying.

The flight to Zurich was uneventful and the fact that it could not be described as comfortable was hardly the airline's fault. It was Lonsdale who insisted that I sat next to Jed and we spent most of the journey fighting for possession of the arm rest between our seats. He wanted it because he was so huge that he needed the space. I wanted it because he wanted it and I didn't want him to feel that he could just push me around easily. I didn't know what was likely to happen in Berne but I did know that if, when the time came for action, he hesitated for just a second then it would be to my advantage.

At Zurich airport the limousine was waiting just as Jeffrey had promised. I got the impression that when Jeffrey said he would do something he did it and guessed that was probably what Lonsdale liked. The chauffeur who came with the limousine handed Jeffrey a packet which Jeffrey put into his briefcase.

CHAPTER THIRTY-EIGHT

The Berne branch of Suisse Credit International is on the Bahnofstrasse, no more than two hundred yards from the railway station.

Like most Swiss banks the emphasis there is all on subtlety and discretion rather than grandeur and show. The entrance to the bank consists of a single rather ordinary looking doorway and the only outside sign of the bank's existence is a highly polished brass plate with the bank's initials on it. If you didn't know there was a bank there and you weren't looking for it you'd never find it.

Inside, the emphasis on discretion became even more obvious. Here the two words that sprang to mind were 'secrecy' and 'paranoia'. There was still no sign that this was a bank. You could have been entering offices occupied by a lawyer or an accountant. The only thing you could tell from the foyer and the reception area was that somewhere, hidden deep behind the oak panelling, there was a lot of money.

Sitting behind a desk the size of a snooker table sat a young man in a dark blue suit. He looked anonymous and had features that made him virtually impossible to describe. Around him the panelling seemed to be uninterrupted until you examined it closely and realised that there were three or four brass door handles fixed into it. A large potted fern sprouted from a dark blue jardiniere to his left. On the young man's right stood an alert and youthful looking guard in a very dark blue uniform. The guard stood virtually to attention and his unbuttoned jacket revealed a shiny, black leather holster with the matt black butt of a revolver peeping from it. My first thought on seeing him was that the unbuttoned jacket gave him a rather slovenly look. My second thought was that the jacket was unbuttoned so that we could see the gun and so that he could reach it.

Lonsdale, followed by Jeffrey, Jed and I, approached the desk.

Lonsdale introduced himself, took a thin leather wallet from his inside jacket pocket, removed a large, engraved visiting card and handed it to the man behind the desk. He treated the young man in the blue suit to one of his rare smiles.

'What can I do for you, sir?'

'I have an appointment to meet a Dr Simpson here,' said Lonsdale. 'He's a colleague of mine and a customer of yours.'

'Just one moment, sir,' said the man in the blue suit. He spoke in perfect English. 'Would you be kind enough to take a seat while I speak to someone who will be able to help you?' He lifted an arm and waved in the direction of a large, brown leather sofa that stretched against most of the oak panelling behind us. He picked up the telephone on his desk, dialled a single digit number and spoke swiftly in Swiss-German, the special language that the Swiss keep to themselves and use when they don't want foreigners to understand what they're talking about.

Lonsdale and Jeffrey sat down on the sofa. Jed stood at one end and glared at the armed guards. After standing for a moment or two I sat down beside Lonsdale. Jeffrey took an international business magazine out of his briefcase and started to read it.

After a minute or two a slight but imposing man in his late sixties came out through one of the doors behind the reception desk. He walked over towards us, peered over half moon spectacles with thin gold frames and spoke to Lonsdale as if he knew who he was. I guessed that there would be closed circuit television cameras hidden somewhere in the panelling.

'My name is Ulrich,' he said. 'I'm the bank's Vice President and Director of Services.' He bowed very slightly after introducing himself. 'I'm afraid that Dr Simpson isn't here at the moment,' he apologised. 'May I ask if there is anything that I or the bank can help you with?' He held his head to one side when he'd finished speaking.

'Have you seen Dr Simpson recently?' Lonsdale asked.

'Well, that's a difficult question to answer,' said Ulrich,

clasping his hands in front of him unhappily. He looked as though he was about to start wringing them.

'I don't understand,' said Lonsdale.

'A Dr Simpson did come into the bank this morning,' said Ulrich. He paused for a moment and swallowed. His adam's apple bobbed up and down furiously. 'But...,' he paused again apparently uncertain about what to say next. He started wringing his hands. 'But it wasn't the right Dr Simpson.'

Lonsdale stared at him, looked at me and then turned and looked at Jeffrey. Then he turned back to Ulrich. 'What do you mean?' he demanded. 'What do you mean, it wasn't the right Dr Simpson?'

Ulrich, busy wringing his hands, seemed desperately upset by all this. A few beads of sweat appeared on his forehead and his adams apple shot up and down several times.

'All our private clients are offered the option of having their accounts ratified with a finger print facility,' said Ulrich.

Lonsdale looked puzzled. He turned to Jeffrey. 'What does he mean?'

Jeffrey licked his lips. 'He means that you can use your finger prints instead of your signature to get access to the account.'

'That's right,' nodded Ulrich. 'It's a security measure that many of our clients find very welcome in these days of...,' he stopped for a moment as though in search of the right word.

'Fraud?' suggested Jeffrey.

Ulrich looked uncomfortable. 'I suppose so,' he agreed. 'Fraud.' He spat the word out as though it made him ill to have it in his mouth.

'And you had a fake Dr Simpson in here this morning?' demanded Lonsdale.

Ulrich nodded. 'A gentleman did attempt to remove money from Dr Simpson's account,' he agreed. 'But,' he added quickly, 'he went away when his fingerprints did not prove to match those registered with the account. He was a fake Dr Simpson.'

'Where did he go?' asked Lonsdale.

'I do not know,' answered Ulrich.

Lonsdale stormed out of the bank. We all followed him.

*　　*　　*

Lonsdale and I sat in a bar together while Jeffrey made

151

telephone calls. Lonsdale had left Jed standing outside the bank in case Dr Simpson turned up. Jeffrey seemed to know a lot of people. After three quarters of an hour he came over to where we were all sitting.

'The real Dr Simpson is here in Berne,' he said. He seemed rather pleased with himself. 'He's registered at The Intercontinental hotel. It's only about two hundred yards away.'

Lonsdale, Jeffrey and I left the bar, climbed into the limousine that was waiting outside and drove the few yards down the road to The Intercontinental. As the car moved away I looked at my watch. I wondered where Michael and Lindsay had got to and how much longer it would be before they were all safely hidden away.

CHAPTER THIRTY-NINE

Simpson was in the lounge of the Intercontinental with a large gin on the table in front of him. To say that he seemed surprised by Lonsdale's arrival would be an understatement.

'What are you doing here?' he blurted out.

Lonsdale glared at him.

Simpson opened his mouth but nothing came out. He shut it again.

'I've got a quiet room on the top floor,' said Jeffrey suddenly appearing by Lonsdale's side. He had a bedroom key in his hand.

Lonsdale still didn't speak. He just stared at Simpson and jerked his head.

'Jerry?' bleated Simpson pitifully. Then, for the first time Simpson saw me standing a couple of yards back. 'What's he doing here?' he demanded. 'It's all his fault!' he said.

Lonsdale moved forwards and put a hand under Simpson's arm. He lifted him to his feet and then half pushed and half pulled him to the bank of elevators on the other side of the lounge.

With the four of us in it the elevator was crowded and I could smell Simpson's fear.

'Do you want me to go and get Jed?' Jeffrey asked.

Lonsdale shook his head. 'I don't need him for this scum,' he said. Those were still the only words he'd uttered since we'd entered the hotel.

The room that Jeffrey had rented was spacious and beautifully furnished. But Jeffrey hadn't booked it so that any of us could relax. As soon as we were all inside Lonsdale locked the door from the inside and pocketed the key.

'I suppose you thought I was going to get put away for a long time,' Lonsdale said to Simpson. Then, suddenly and without warning he slapped the doctor's face. Simpson seemed stunned by surprise as much as by pain.

'Jerry!' he persisted. 'Jerry, let's talk. I didn't open the account. It wasn't anything to do with me.'

'What is there to talk about?' asked Lonsdale through tight lips. He hit Simpson again, this time with the back of his hand. The heavy signet ring that he wore cut Simpson's cheek and left him splattered with blood. 'Except the money,' he added.

'I only came to get the money,' said Simpson. 'Our money.' He tried to add something. 'I couldn't...,' he started to say. But Lonsdale wasn't in the mood for listening. He hit Simpson again but this time he hit him with his clenched fist. Simpson's head rocked backwards and he lost his balance and fell heavily onto the floor. He lay there, unmoving. His breathing had become loud and laboured.

'Get up!' snarled Lonsdale, kicking his partner in the stomach.

Simpson's body jerked involuntarily and he seemed to be trying to stand up. Then suddenly he lurched forward, clutching at his chest. His breathing became more difficult, he started to sweat and his skin turned grey. Then he fell forward onto his face. I found it impossible to feel pity for him. This time he didn't move any more.

Lonsdale bent down and tried to lift him but the doctor had become a dead weight.

'Oh, shit,' murmured Jeffrey, quietly and almost inaudibly. He bent down and lifted Simpson's head. 'You've killed him!' He picked up one of Simpson's hands. '£25 million in the bank and without his finger prints you can't get a penny of it.'

Lonsdale's face drained of colour.

'You knew he had high blood pressure,' observed Jeffrey. It may have been meant as a simple statement of fact but it was the first time I'd heard Jeffrey say anything remotely critical to Lonsdale.

Shocked, Lonsdale sat down on the edge of the bed. Jeffrey stood up and moved away from the body. He scratched his forehead. He seemed to be trying to decide what to do next.

'Maybe we could cut a finger off and take it in with us...,' said Lonsdale.

'Great idea,' said Jeffrey, sarcastically. 'I'm sure the bank would love that.'

Lonsdale put his head in his hands. He stayed like that for what seemed to be an hour or two. It was probably a minute. Maybe two minutes. Then, slowly, he moved. 'What name did you book this room under?' Lonsdale asked suddenly.

Jeffrey looked at him. 'Yours.' he said. He looked down at Simpson's body again. 'I didn't think anything...' His voice faded and he shrugged.

Lonsdale swore repeatedly. 'If you'd used another name we could have just walked out of here and left him.'

'If you hadn't hit him so hard he wouldn't be dead,' countered Jeffrey.

Neither of them seemed to be aware that I was still in the room. Slowly, I started to move towards the door.

Lonsdale looked up and saw me moving. 'Where do you think you're going?'

'I thought I'd go and see the sights,' I said. 'I've never been to Berne before.'

'You're staying here,' screamed Lonsdale. He lunged at me. He wasn't a particularly strong man and I pushed him aside easily. I'd have been more worried if Jed had been in the room. But Jed was still standing outside the bank down the road.

Lonsdale tried to grab my arm but he was like a kid fighting in the playground. I jabbed him in the chest. He stood there for a moment coughing and spluttering. Jeffrey hadn't moved.

'What's the point of staying here?' I asked. 'You've got enough problems without worrying about me.' I nodded towards Simpson lying on the floor. 'You've got to do something about Simpson's body and you can't get the money out of the bank because Simpson is dead.'

Lonsdale looked to Jeffrey for help.

'He's right,' nodded Jeffrey, who seemed remarkably calm. 'He's just a bloody nuisance now.' He put his hand into his jacket pocket and pulled out a small automatic.

'Where the hell did you get that from?' demanded Lonsdale, surprised.

'The chauffeur,' explained Jeffrey. Then he shot Lonsdale through the heart. The gun made a quiet 'phut'.

I stared disbelievingly.

155

'What a mess,' said Jeffrey quietly. 'What a terrible, bloody mess.'

I just stood there and stared, first at him, then at Lonsdale, then at Simpson.

Jeffrey didn't seem concerned. He wiped the automatic and then crossed the room and carefully pressed the gun into Simpson's right hand.

I watched.

'Simple really,' he said. 'The two of them had a row. Simpson shot him,' he nodded at Lonsdale, 'and then in all the excitement had a heart attack and died.'

I didn't say anything.

'You're the only loose end,' he said. 'What do I do with you?'

'Why do anything with me? I'm not going to talk to anyone.'

Jeffrey thought for a moment.

'If you kill me the scenario gets screwed up a bit,' I argued. 'These two are business partners but what am I doing here?'

Jeffrey nodded slowly.

'And if you take me with you I'll be a real drag,' I went on. I paused. 'Even if you could take me with you,' I added with what I hoped was a smile.

Jeffrey just stared.

'If you worked for Lonsdale why did you kill him?'

'I didn't work for Lonsdale,' Jeffrey said. He looked offended. 'I work for people in the States. My people have been using Lonsdale's nursing homes as an investment.'

'Ah! You're in the laundry business!'

Jeffrey didn't answer. 'They won't be pleased to hear that Lonsdale screwed up,' he said. 'It was a good operation.' He looked at me sharply. 'I don't suppose you have any idea who the fake Dr Simpson was?'

I ignored him. 'What about the £25 million?' I asked. 'They won't like losing all that money will they?'

He nodded towards the two bodies on the floor. 'That was their money,' he said. 'My bosses wouldn't let jerks like Lonsdale and Simpson control the organisation's cash.' He shrugged and stared down at Simpson. 'Pity,' he said. He nodded towards Simpson. 'He was the only guy who could get the damned money out and I can hardly drag him into the bank to use his fingerprints can I?' He looked rueful. 'Pity,' he said again.

I said nothing and kept still.

Jeffrey stared at me. 'You're not going to talk, are you?'

I shook my head.

Jeffrey stared at me. 'Then piss off. I'll give you five minutes then I'm off too. You leave by the front door. I'm going out by the back.'

I headed for the room door and turned with my hand on the doorknob. 'One thing,' I said, 'I don't know how good the Swiss police are but Simpson was left handed.' I nodded towards the gun. 'One good turn and all that.'

Jeffrey stared at me and then nodded. For a few seconds I thought he was going to smile but he didn't. 'Thanks!' was all he said. The last thing I saw as I left the room was him bending down and moving the gun from Simpson's right hand to his left.

I thought it was nice of him to trust me and then I left. On the train back to Zurich I wondered how long Jed would wait outside the bank.

CHAPTER FORTY

I stood for a few moments just staring out of the bedroom window. Even though it was still not seven o'clock I had to use my hand to shade my eyes from the early morning sun. Just below my window half a dozen visitors were already sitting having breakfast at the white metal tables set out in the tiny courtyard. Half a dozen wizened olive trees provided a little shade.

One side of the courtyard was bordered by a low, white stone wall and beyond that I could see the sea crashing against the rocky shore. There was no wind and as they collapsed upon the rocks the waves seemed exhausted by their journey around the Mediterranean.

I was about to get dressed when I remembered that the only clothes I'd brought with me were the ones I'd been wearing. I went into the bathroom and found a white towelling bathrobe hanging behind the door. I put it on and went downstairs to the reception desk.

The hotel shop wasn't yet open but the receptionist found the key and let me choose a pair of shorts, a pair of simple, canvas sandals and a pair of sunglasses. I paid by credit card and then went back up to my room to dress.

I breakfasted on orange juice, freshly baked rolls and two soft boiled eggs then I wandered down a flight of weathered stone steps to the beach. There I settled down between two rocks from where I could see both the sea and the entrance to the hotel. I half closed my eyes and allowed myself to daydream.

Lindsay took centre stage and I could remember our delight when we had first found this small hotel. It had been even smaller then; no annexe, no restaurant, no shop. And much

158

cheaper. But the sun was the same, the sea was the same and the beach was unchanged.

We had been travelling around Europe for three weeks. We had started in France, worked our way down through Italy and travelled across to the Greek mainland by steamer. From there we had taken a small ferry to the first of the Greek islands. The island of Cos had been the fifth island we had visited and we had loved it so much that we had stayed there until it was time to go back home. They were happy days. Mornings spent swimming in the clear, blue waters around the island. Afternoons spent lying around talking, reading and soaking up the sun. Evenings spent eating, drinking and dancing.

After a week we'd come perilously close to running out of money and had thought we would have to start hitching our way back home.

But a fellow called Dimitrios, who ran the local café, heard of our cash flow problems and offered us both part time jobs. He had bought an old refrigerator and a few gallons of ice cream and wanted us to set up an ice cream stall outside the café. The idea was that we would take it in turns to run the stall but we didn't want to be separated so we worked together for a few hours every day.

The tubs in which the ice cream came were marked with a dozen different labels and should have contained Pistachio, Coffee, Chocolate, Peach, Raspberry and Lime flavours. But somewhere along the line someone had messed up the filling process and all we had was strawberry ice cream. It didn't seem to matter. No one seemed to care. People who wanted ice cream didn't seem to mind what flavour they got.

We finally left the island and we both cried when we parted at Gatwick airport. We had to go back to our respective universities but swore that we would see one another as much as possible. I don't remember what went wrong. We both got involved in our studies and had less and less time for travelling. Slowly, we drifted apart.

I heard a taxi screech to a halt and looked up towards the hotel. Four weary visitors clambered out of the dust cloud. I recognised them at once. They stood still for a moment while the taxi driver opened the boot of the car and removed their bags. Running up from the beach I waved and called Lindsay's name.

Moments later we were wrapped in one another's arms.

CHAPTER FORTY-ONE

The five of us were sitting on rocks by the water's edge. Lizzie was dangling her feet in the water. Barbara and Michael were sitting holding hands. Lindsay and I were sharing a strawberry ice cream which we'd bought from a boy who was operating an ice cream truck parked a hundred yards from the beach. I had explained to them all exactly what had happened. I thought they had a right to know.

'It sounds a terrible thing to say,' said Michael, 'but I'm glad they're both dead.'

'It's not a terrible thing to say,' said Lizzie, kicking her feet in the water. 'They were both horrible.'

'And if they hadn't died then they would have probably carried on with business as usual!' Barbara pointed out. 'I don't think any of us could have lived with that.'

Michael shook his head.

Lindsay held the ice cream cornet up high and allowed a few drops of pink ice cream to drip into her mouth. She pressed her lips against its coolness and closed her eyes.

'I guess we can go back to London whenever we like now?' said Lizzie, half turning.

'Yes,' I nodded. 'I got Lindsay to bring you here because I didn't know what Lonsdale would do. I wanted you somewhere safe.'

Lindsay fed me the remains of her ice cream cone. Then she dipped her sticky fingers into the sea and washed them.

'It's lovely and warm,' she said. Suddenly, without warning, she stood up and dived into the sea. She disappeared into the warm waters of the mediterranean with hardly a ripple. As she surfaced she shook her head and rubbed at her eyes with her fingers. She had been wearing a thin, white cotton dress when she dived in. She trod water for a while as she unfastened the buttons at the back. Then she dived and wriggled and a few moments later held up the dress. Taking careful aim she threw it straight at me. I ducked to one side and it landed on the rock behind me. 'Come on in!' she shouted.

I took off my sandals, then took the wallet out of my shorts pocket and put it alongside them. Then I dived in.

'Race you!' shouted Lindsay. She was already swimming towards the other side of the small bay.

I beat her by a length, pulled myself out of the water, waved to Michael, Barbara and Lizzie and then helped pull Lindsay out of the water so that she could sit on the rock beside me.

'It's wonderful to be back,' Lindsay said quietly. She slipped her arm around me and kissed me on the cheek.

I put my arm around her and kissed her.

'Is it all over now?' she asked.

'Yes. The people who were funding Lonsdale won't make a fuss. They want it all to die down as soon as possible. Someone will buy the nursing homes.'

There was a silence. 'Can I ask you something?' asked Lindsay.

'Of course!' I said. 'But I want to ask you something too.' I warned her.

'Who was the other Dr Simpson?' Lindsay asked. 'Who was the man who called at the bank and tried to get at Simpson's money. I don't understand that.'

I grinned at her. 'There wasn't anyone else,' I told her. 'The man who called at the bank was Dr Simpson.'

Lindsay looked puzzled. 'I don't understand,' she said. 'If it was him why didn't his finger prints match? Why couldn't he get the money out?'

'Because I set up the account,' I explained. 'The account can only be operated with my finger prints.'

Lindsay stared at me.

'I flew out to Zurich,' I told her. 'I opened an account in Zurich under the name of Dr Simpson. Then I transferred the money to Berne by telephone so that no one at the bank would be able to recognise me.'

Lindsay looked puzzled.

'I wanted three things,' I explained. 'First, I wanted to hide their money somewhere that they couldn't get hold of it. Second, I wanted to make Lonsdale think that Simpson had run off with the money so that they would start mistrusting one another. And, finally, I wanted a little insurance. If the worst happened I wanted to be able to tell them that they needed me alive to get at their money.' I paused. 'I intended to tell them where the money was,' I said. I shrugged. 'But they both died.'

'So you're the only person who can get into the account?'

I nodded.

'Over twenty million pounds?'

Another nod.

'And no one else knows it's there?'

'No.'

Lindsay was silent for a moment. 'What are you going to do with it?'

'I don't know.'

Lindsay said nothing for a few moments. 'Can they do anything about the fact that you used a false name?'

I shook my head.

'Didn't they want to see any identification?'

'I showed them an identity card I had made at the airport,' I told her. 'It has my photograph on together with the name Simpson. And it's covered in plastic. It looks very official.'

Slowly Lindsay stared to laugh. She looked at me. 'Did you ever think that this would happen?'

'No.' I said instantly and honestly. 'I assumed that as soon as Barbara and Lizzie were free I'd just give them back their money.' I paused. 'I didn't count on them being killed.'

We both said nothing for a while but just relaxed in the sunshine.

'Do you have to rush back to England?' I asked her.

'No,' said Lindsay. 'Do you?'

'No.'

'Is that what you wanted to ask me?'

'What?'

'Whether I had to rush back to England? You said that there was something you had to ask me.'

'Oh, no,' I said. 'That wasn't it. Do you remember when we spoke together last on the phone?'

'Yes.'

'You said something at the end. I didn't hear it properly.'

Lindsay nodded and grinned at me. 'I remember,' she said softly.

'What was it?' I asked her.

'What was what?' she said, teasing.

'What did you say?'

She moved closer and whispered in my ear.

I smiled, held her tighter and kissed her lightly on the lips. She put her arms around my neck, pulled me towards her and kissed me back more firmly.

After a few moments we parted and Lindsay shivered. A slight breeze was building up and waves were beginning to crash noisily onto the rocks around us. I lowered my head and whispered to her again. She laughed gently and kissed me.

Also Published by Chilton Designs

THE BILBURY CHRONICLES
Vernon Colman

The first in the Bilbury series of novels describing the adventures (and misadventures) of a young doctor who enters general practice as the assistant to an elderly and rather eccentric doctor in North Devon.

When he arrives in Bilbury, a small village on the edge of Exmoor, the young doctor doesn't realise how much he has to learn. And he soon discovers the true extent of his ignorance when he meets his patients.

There's Anne Thwaites who gives birth to her first baby in a field; Thumper Robinson who knows a few tricks that aren't in any textbook and Mike Trickle, a TV quiz show host who causes great excitement when he buys a house in the village.

Then there's elderly Dr Brownlow himself who lives in a house that looks like a castle, drives an old Rolls Royce and patches his stethoscope with a bicycle inner tube repair kit; Frank the inebriate landlord of the Duck and Puddle, and Peter who runs the local taxi, delivers the mail and works as the local undertaker.

There's Miss Johnson, the receptionist with a look that can curdle milk; Mrs Wilson the buxom district nurse and Len her husband who is the local policeman with an embarrassing secret.

'A delightful read. I was entranced for hours.'

Miss S, Devon

'I loved this book. Please send two more copies as soon as possible.'
Mrs S, Nottingham

'Wonderful. One of the best novels I've ever read.'
Mr T, Leamington Spa

'I enjoyed "The Bilbury Chronicles" more than any other book I've read for years. I am very much looking forward to the sequel.'
Mrs G, Sunderland

ISBN 0 9503527 5 6   230 pages   £12.95

BILBURY GRANGE
Vernon Coleman

The second novel in the Bilbury series. The Doctor and his wife move to Bilbury Grange – a dream of a house with stone lions guarding the front door, a Victorian, walled kitchen garden and a coach house complete with clocktower. But the newly married couple have no idea of the horrors that await them – crumbling slates, rampant woodworm, creeping dry rot and, worst of all, crooked builders all too ready to lend a hand. With money tight and repair bills soaring the young couple have to find a way to make ends meet.

But repairing Bilbury Grange isn't the only problem they face. Rumours abound that a developer is about to build new houses and a golf course in the village – and to top it all Thumper Robinson gets arrested!

Somewhere, as all this is going on, the Doctor and Patsy find time to adopt two young kittens and four young lambs.

'Captures the essence of old-fashioned village life where you never needed to lock your door.'

Western Evening Herald

'A wonderful book for relaxing and unwinding . . . makes you want to up roots and move to the rural heartland.'

Lincolnshire Echo

'For sheer relaxing pleasure here's another witty tale from the doctor whose prolific writings are so well known to many of us.'

Bookshelf

ISBN 0 9503527 7 2   247 pages   £12.95

BILBURY REVELS
Vernon Coleman

The Bilbury series continues with this, the third novel set in the idyllic Exmoor village.

Disaster strikes during a long, relentless storm which batters Bilbury Grange, cuts off the village and blankets the whole area in a thick covering of snow. The Doctor nearly loses his life (he is saved by his faithful dog Ben) and the village schoolteacher loses her cottage roof.

The fun really starts when the villagers join together to raise money to repair the devastated cottage. Vernon Coleman describes an old-fashioned music hall evening (during which just about everything which can go wrong does go wrong), one of the funniest cricket matches ever to take place, and a village Produce Show where the locals compete (with some very surprising results) to find out who has grown the biggest and best vegetables.

And as if that wasn't enough the Doctor has to promote his first book. He travels to London, makes his first hilarious television appearance, and is invited to speak at a local village hall where things aren't quite what they seem to be.

Vernon Coleman's comic novels have been compared to Jerome K. Jerome's classic 'Three Men in a Boat'. Readers of the previous Bilbury books will love The Bilbury Revels. New readers be warned – you'll be hooked.

'How I enjoyed the first two Bilbury books. Dr Coleman is a superb author. Will you please inform me when the fourth Bilbury is available – not soon enough for me.'

Mrs Y, Plymouth

ISBN 1 898146 05 5   270 pages   £12.95

THE VILLAGE CRICKET TOUR
Vernon Coleman

A novel describing the adventures and mishaps of a team of cricketers who spend two weeks of their summer holidays on a cricket tour of the West Country, and who make up in enthusiasm for what they may lack in skill.

'If anyone ever manages to bottle the essence of the village cricket he will very quickly scale the dizzy heights of personal fortune. In the meantime we read and write about it in pursuit of understanding. Seminal reading here includes Selincourt and Blunden and should now embrace Vernon Coleman's latest offering, a whimsical piece about the peregrinations of a village team on its summer tour . . . all the characters are here, woven together by a raft of anecdotes and reminiscences and a travelogue of some of the most picturesque spots in the south west.'

The Cricketer

'Describes in hilarious fashion the triumphs and disasters of a Midlands team's tour of the West Country and there is not a little of Jerome K. Jerome in Mr Coleman's style.'

Worcester Evening News

'I enjoyed it immensely. He has succeeded in writing a book that will entertain, a book that will amuse and warm the cockles of tired hearts. And what a change it makes from the wearisome cluckings of the current crop of cricket books with their grinding pomposity and, in many cases, their staggering lack of craftsmanship and originality.'

Punch

'A delightful book which also highlights some of the most spectacular scenery in Cornwall and Devon.'

The Cornishman

'Vernon Coleman is obviously a man who has enjoyed his cricket and over the years has committed to memory the many characters he has seen playing the game. He weaves them into the story as he charts the progress of his team's tour of Devon and Cornwall. The tale captures club cricket as everyone imagines it should be.'

Falmouth Packet

'Coleman is a very funny writer. It would be a pity if cricketers were the only people to read this book.'

This England

ISBN 0 9503527 3 X   173 pages   £9.95

THE MAN WHO INHERITED A GOLF COURSE
Vernon Coleman

Trevor Dukinfield, the hero of this delightful novel, is a young, not very successful journalist. Completely out of the blue, Trevor receives a letter informing him that he has inherited a golf course from an uncle he never knew he had.

You might think that this would have been greeted by Trevor as good news. Indeed, Trevor *did* treat it as good news until he heard about the two small snags which accompanied his good fortune.

First, in order to keep the golf club under the rules of his uncle's will, Trevor must play a round of golf in less than 100 strokes. Second, he has to find a partner to help him beat two bankers in a match play competition.

Not particularly stringent conditions you might think – except that Trevor has never played a round of golf in his life, unless you count an hour spent on a crazy golf course in Weston-super-Mare.

'*Another witty volume from the doctor who has successfully turned from medical topics to novel writing. The . . . mix of anecdotes and moments of sheer farce make for an absorbing read.*'

Lancashire Evening Telegraph

'*. . . another delightful and amusing story. I rate this one as the best of his twelve novels so far. His fans will lap it up.*'

Sunday Independent

ISBN 0 9503527 9 9   237 pages   £12.95

ALICE'S DIARY
The Memoirs of a Cat

Alice is a mixed tabby cat whose first book sparkles with wit and fun and a rare enthusiasm for life. Whether she is describing her relationship with human beings with whom she shares her life (there are two of them – described as the Upright in Trousers and the Upright who wears a Skirt), her relationships with her many cat friends or her (not always successful) attempts at hunting, no cat lover will fail to find her story enchanting. Most important, every reader will, for the first time, have an insight into what it is really like to be a cat.

Extracts from some of the hundreds of letters received:

'I have just finished reading "Alice's Diary" and what a delight it was. We have three cats and I can say with all honesty that I could have been reading about them.'

Mrs W, Cheshire

'I have just received my copy of "Alice's Diary" and really did enjoy every page. I have recommended it to several of my friends.'

Mrs C, London

'Each night I read one month of your diary to my husband and all three of our cats came to listen as well!'

Mrs G, Berkshire

'Please send copies of "Alice's Diary" to the eleven friends on the accompanying list. It is a wonderful book that will give them all great pleasure.'

Mr R, Lancashire

'A delightful book. I thoroughly enjoyed it.'

Mr W, Midlands

"Alice's Diary" is one of the nicest books I have ever read. She has wonderful insight. When do we get the next instalment? I can hardly wait. It really is an enchanting book.'

Mrs J, London

ISBN 0 9503527 1 3   142 pages   £9.95

ALICE'S ADVENTURES
The Further Memoirs of a Cat

After the publication of her first book Alice was inundated with fan mail urging her to put pen to paper once more. The result is this, her second volume of memoirs.

No one could have predicted what was to happen to Alice during this, the most eventful year of her life.

Alice's Adventures is full of the wry and witty observations which delighted the readers of her first book. The wonderful illustrations accurately capture the most poignant moments throughout the year.

Another must for cat lovers everywhere.

'I didn't think Alice could surpass her first book – but she has. I really loved "Alice's Adventures". The saddest moment came when I finished it. When will the next volume be ready?'

Mrs K, Somerset

'We have had cats for 30 years and Alice describes incidents that are so real that we nearly died laughing at them'.

Mrs O, Leeds

"Alice's Adventures" is the loveliest book I have ever read. It captures everything brilliantly. Thinking back over the book I can't help smiling. I have never enjoyed a book as much.'

Mrs H, Edinburgh

'What a wonderful book. It was a real pleasure to read.'

Mr E, Exeter

'Delighted with Alice's Diary, must have Alice's Adventures!'

Mrs J, Derby

ISBN 0 9503527 6 4   133 pages   £9.95

MRS CALDICOT'S CABBAGE WAR
Vernon Coleman

Thelma Caldicot was married to her husband for thirty dull and boring years. Then completely out of the blue, two police officers arrived at Thelma's house to break some sad news. That afternoon, while her husband was at a cricket match, she had become a widow.

Her ambitious son Derek soon appears on the scene, determined to interfere in every aspect of his mother's life. After thirty years of being dominated by her husband, it looks as though Thelma's son is about to step into his shoes and continue the good work.

But then something happens to Thelma Caldicot. After years of being pushed around and told what to do, she takes charge of her life and fights back.

Mrs Caldicot's Cabbage War is the poignant, warm and often funny story of an ordinary women who finally decides to stand up for herself.

'. . . a splendid, relaxing read . . .'   *Sunday Independent*

'I am reading "Mrs Caldicot" at present and enjoying it immensely. Thank you'

Mrs C, Darwen

'Thank you so much for "Mrs Caldicot's Cabbage War". All your books are great.'

Mrs N, Surrey

ISBN 0 9503527 8 0   150 pages   £9.95

THOMAS WINSDEN'S CRICKETING ALMANACK
Edited by Vernon Coleman

A spoof of the cricketing 'bible' Wisden.

Thomas Winsden was born in 1811 in the village of Headingley and later moved with his family to London. Unfortunate family circumstances, and the untimely death of his father meant that the young Thos Winsden found himself in charge of his brothers and sisters as well as his grieving mother. Fired with a sense of responsibility he started to write a cricketing almanack which was intended to be the foundation of his publishing empire. Sadly his dreams were not fulfilled and although the Almanack was written each year, it was never published despite the best efforts of the Winsden family.

In 1982 the last member of the Winsden family died and, as luck would have it, Vernon Coleman was on hand to take over the production of the Cricketing Almanack. At last Vernon Coleman has made this important and hysterically funny sporting book available to the general public.

The 136th edition of Thomas Winsden's Cricketing Almanack contains gems such as:

Etiquette for Spectators
What Umpires Carry in their Pockets
Ten Unforgettable Scorers
The Ten Most Interesting Slow Bowlers of all Time
How to Clap
Women's Cricket Comes of Age
The World Beach Cricket Championships
Food and Drink for the Cricketer

Illustrated. A must for all cricket-lovers everywhere!

ISBN 1 898146 00 4   128 pages   £9.95

If you would like to receive information about our new publications and special offers then please send your name and address to:

Chilton Designs Publishers
PO Box 47
Barnstaple
Devon
EX32 8YT